TOMORROW DETECTIVE

A TIME TRAVEL DETECTIVE MYSTERY

NATHAN VAN COOPS

Skylighter
Press

For the ones who forgive.

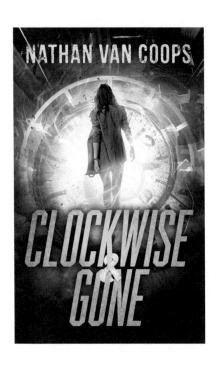

Get a free time travel novella when you join the newsletter for books by Nathan Van Coops. Get your free book here: https://BookHip.com/DLSLZMV

PART 1
CASSIUS

CHAPTER 1

Cassius. 1984. Fifteen Minutes After Midnight

Cassius Roseland sat on the edge of his bar stool unable to ignore the knot in his stomach. He looked at his hands instead. They hadn't come clean. The deepest creases of his knuckles revealed the dirt. It was under his nails too. Maybe that was a good thing. Might have stopped some of the blood from getting under there.

But he could still smell it.

The weight of the .45 in his waistband made his pants heavy. He put a hand to the fold of his shirt covering the gun. He should have gotten rid of it by now. But he didn't know what new danger might be coming for him. He'd need something to protect himself.

His hand was still shaking. He tried putting it in his sweatshirt pocket but recoiled at the cold metal still in there. The watch.

"You decide what you're having?"

The bartender was back. The knockout blonde with the kind eyes.

"Uh, rum and Coke?"

She nodded and reached for a glass.

At least they had Coke here. Hard to tell since the place looked like Sherlock Holmes might walk in any minute. Maybe Robin Hood. Bunch of old wood and antique glass. Tough to put a time to any of it. Maybe that was the point. A signed baseball sat on a shelf behind the bar though. That was something.

There was a band in the corner, two girls plucking away at guitars and a twiggy little dude on a keyboard. Music was pretty out there. The girls were singing to each other like they needed to get a room.

Cassius checked his watch again.

Where the hell was she?

He reached into his rear pants pocket and felt the code cards. His ticket out. This would all be for nothing if he hadn't kept those. He scanned the half-filled pub. No one was looking at him now, but they were when he wasn't watching. He could feel it. Did they know what he'd done? Maybe they could tell. Maybe they could smell the blood too. But no one was saying anything. A little longer and he'd be free.

The bartender pushed his drink toward him. "Are you a new guest?"

"Yeah," Cassius replied. "When do we leave?"

"Inn just got here. Have to wait for all the guests to check in."

"So, like an hour, or what?"

"In a rush for your vacation? Starts with relaxing, you know."

Cassius unclenched his fist and reached for the drink. His hand still trembled but not so bad. "You're right. Just gotta get that chill attitude, huh?"

The bartender moved off to help another guest but her green eyes had lingered on his for too long, hadn't they?

How could she know? He looked himself over again. Just his fresh black jeans, tee, and his lucky sleeveless fight hoodie. He was clean enough. But that's when he spotted the flecks of blood on his shoes.

He spilled some of the drink on himself.

"Shit," he muttered as he reached for some napkins.

Someone came in the door as he was wiping at his Converse and he started again. But it was just the short Latin guy with the mustache he'd met in the hall.

He needed to calm down. Everything was fine. In a few minutes she'd be here. Then this place would vanish like he'd seen it arrive. They'd be safe from Mickey. Safe from the cops, far away from–

The door opened again. The figure stepped through and his heart sank.

Kid was still wearing the same jacket. Now bloodstained and filthy. He was just a skinny teenager, and looked it even more in this light. Needed twenty pounds to make middleweight. But the night had aged him. He had blood in his hair. Nothing about those blue eyes looked like a kid anymore. All ice. Hate too.

Cassius slid his hand to his waist and up under his sweatshirt. His fingers wrapped around the grip of the .45.

How'd this kid find him? The hell was he doing here?

The room grew quiet. All eyes fixed on the two of them.

Couldn't he have left it alone, just for tonight?

But the question rang false in Cassius's brain. He knew why he'd come. What it must mean about the girl from the sidewalk.

If someone had done what he'd done, he'd follow them to the ends of the earth too.

This was it.

He never should have taken this job. Never should have got in the car tonight. For sure never should have done what he did to that girl. But what's done was done.

The kid had both hands in his jacket pockets. What did he have in there? It didn't matter. He was what? Sixteen?

Seventeen? Cassius had ten years on him. He'd stared down plenty of tougher punks in the ring over the years. Kid would back down for sure if he saw the .45 again. What was he going to do, shout at him in front of all these people? That's not how it was done.

He'd back down.

But there went his way out. Could that pretty blonde see to letting him stay after running some kid off with a gun?

She'd have to. He'd make her. It was the only way.

At least the kid hadn't brought any cops. His mistake.

Cassius slid off his stool.

Dumb kid was just standing there, staring him down.

"You don't want none of this," Cassius said. "Get gone."

But the kid didn't blink. He took two steps closer instead and squared up. Maybe ten feet between them now.

Cassius set his jaw. Blood was pounding in his ears. Had his adrenaline ever come down tonight?

He'd keep his finger off the trigger this time. Just a little show.

"I said get out!" he shouted and yanked the .45 loose from his waistband.

The pinch came at the same time as the pop, twisting him off balance. But it was the second shot that he saw. Stuffing from inside that jacket flew out. Kid had blown a hole clean through his pocket.

Cassius looked down. The second thump. That had hurt more.

Was this what that girl had felt?

He staggered backward, hit the stool. Shit.

He sat.

The .45 fell from his hand and clattered to the floor. What a dumb thing to do. Cassius felt the urge to apologize to the rest of the pub. He reached for the gun, but lost his footing. He hit the floor with his knees, then his face. He felt his nose break.

Someone kicked his gun away from his fingertips.

Shouting.

He rolled over.

The kid loomed over him, the gun in plain sight now. He bent and picked something up off the floor. That damned watch.

"This isn't yours."

Cassius let his head fall back. Blood from his nose was getting in his mouth.

Here came that blonde again, leaning over him. She had a towel, and blood on her hands. His blood. But it wasn't from his face.

He stared up at the wooden beams of the ceiling. He would have really liked to see it all disappear like they said it would. That would have been some vacation.

CHAPTER 2

Greyson. 2035. Fourteen Years Later.

"Your beer is getting warm."

I looked up from the tavern jump schedule I'd been staring at and found the woman speaking. She was new. Must be a guest.

"I'm letting it breathe," I said. "Some beer needs a little time to achieve its full potential."

"Don't we all." The young woman had an easy smile. Pretty. Her dark hair was recently braided. "You're a guest too?" She indicated the stool next to me and I nodded. She slid onto it.

"Sort of a hitchhiker at the moment," I said.

"I'm Nadia."

"Greyson."

"Looked like you were pondering deep thoughts, Greyson."

"All for show," I said. "I'm shockingly shallow."

She laughed. It was a nice laugh. Nice figure. Nice everything really. A little young for me, but the kind of woman I wouldn't mind having to sit next to most nights.

I sipped my warm beer and tried to wash down memories of the past.

"God, she's so nice, isn't she?" Nadia said. She was looking down the bar to where Heavens Archer was chatting with another guest. "And I'd kill for those legs."

"Don't try to run with her. The woman is a springbok."

"Advice noted. You two are friends?"

I sipped my beer again. That was a question I didn't have an answer for. For several weeks Heavens and I had been making sparks in each other's proximity, but nothing had caught fire. But the last few days she'd been distant. Not that I noticed those kinds of things.

"Coworkers. Sort of."

"Oh, you work here too?" Nadia asked. "That must be a trip. And you get to drink on the job."

"My help is more of an 'as needed' capacity."

"Mysterious."

"What about you, Nadia? Vacation?"

"Accomplishing a long-awaited life goal," she said.

Heavens chose that moment to approach. "Nadia, welcome. Assume you found your room okay. Can I get you something?"

"The room is perfect. And I'll have whatever he's having."

"You've met Greyson, I see."

"We're pretending to be deep people together."

"Greyson might surprise you," Heavens said, glancing at me for the first time. Her green eyes held mine. "He has all kinds of secrets."

The spark was there again, and the room cooled ten degrees when she looked away.

Heavens poured Nadia's beer, then walked to the other end of the bar.

Nadia turned to me and arched an eyebrow. "*Just* coworkers?"

I shrugged. The hell if I knew.

"Here's to secrets then." She held up her glass.

I clinked mine against it. "Cheers." I took another sip, but she was right. It was too warm. Breathing hadn't helped. I set the beer on the bar and got off my stool. "Pleasure meeting you, Nadia."

"Okay. See ya," she said, disappointment creeping in.

I walked out of the pub's swinging doors and into the lobby of the inn. A few new arrivals were milling about. It was easy to spot time travel tourists. Most either wore the clothing styles of their native decades or were trying too hard to fit in with looks from the past. The gaggle of middle-aged guests approaching the pub doors looked like a disco had thrown up on them. One guy wore glittery gloves and an early Michael Jackson perm.

I took a left at the stairs and climbed.

The halls of the Rose 'n Bridge meandered in a way many found charming. I only wished for a straight path to my room. But no one ever asked me. Fortunately, I reached the end of my hallway and had my key out without having to contend with any coherent thoughts. I paused near my doorway. A white rose was lying on the floor. Just a single stem and flower.

It was in the center of the hall, so I bent and picked it up. No doubt another admirer of Heavens. Her door was directly across from mine. Wasn't the first time someone had felt compelled to leave her a token of their affection. Not like I should care either. I had no claim on her. She'd said as much.

But if you are going to leave a goddess a rose, you should give it some damn water. I opened my door and entered the room that had been home for the last few weeks. I sliced the tip of the flower stem off with my pocketknife and searched the cabinets of my kitchenette. A pint glass would do. I filled it from the tap and plunked the rose into it. Then I walked back out and left it by Heavens' door.

I shut my own door again and breathed in the silence.

Something chimed in my jacket pocket.

I sighed. Couldn't even get silence right today.

My phone had a notification. Secure text.

>>> WE NEED TO TALK

The name got my attention. Captain Jonathan Black Elk.

It had been a long time. He'd given me temporal coordinates to contact him with.

I put my earpiece in and pressed the call button.

The phone made a series of clicks as it routed through the inn's tachyon pulse transmitter and across time.

The other end picked up.

"Temporal Crimes Investigation Division." The voice sounded tired.

"It's Greyson Travers. Got your message."

The long pause at the other end made me wonder if we'd been disconnected. Finally he spoke again. "Wanted to call you personally. Promised I would."

My chest tightened.

"Been fourteen years for both of you. They're letting him out."

"He was supposed to have six more." I didn't intend it to come out as a growl but it did.

"He cooperated in an important investigation for Financial Crimes. Guys we've been after for a long time. Valuable information. Plus good behavior."

"Doesn't make up for what he did."

"Nothing will."

I walked to the kitchen table and sat. "Where is he?"

"A timeline not far from his original. Parole requires no time devices. Linear time gap to make the fourteen years easier to adjust to. Fresh start. He's moving on with his life. You should too."

"Who else knows he's out?"

"Besides TCID? You. We plan to keep it that way. Old grudges die hard. They should die though, Greyson."

11

"I see him, I'm not making any promises."

Black Elk sighed. "You both got off easy all those years ago. Him surviving. You being underage. Plus enough witnesses saw him draw on you first. But you and I both know you didn't walk into that tavern looking to have a peaceful chat."

"No comment."

"I don't want to hear about this blowing up again, Grey. The past is the past."

"Everyone's past is someone's future."

"Better not be yours."

The line disconnected.

I put my phone away, then walked back into the hallway to stare at the white rose in the pint glass.

Then I kicked it over.

CHAPTER 3

Cassius. 1984. 25 Minutes earlier.

His breath was ragged. His sneakers pounded the pavement as he ran. He ignored the stares of people he passed on the sidewalks and just clung to the strap of the bag over his shoulder. He paused at a corner and caught sight of himself in the storefront window. His eyes were those of a wild animal. Calm down. Calm down.

No. He had to keep going.

He looked at the strange watch in his palm. His hand was shaking. He shoved the watch into his sweatshirt pocket and ran on.

The street signs counted down. He was getting closer.

He dug in his other pockets and pulled out the wallet he'd taken off Johnny. Checked the address on the card. He turned left, and slowed some, walking the last block.

Then he was there. But nothing else was. He stared.

It was just a construction site. Chain link fencing blocked access, and netting on the fence obstructed the view. No building. It was a tall fence, but it couldn't hide a whole building, could it?

He checked his Casio. Shit. Was he too late? Had he missed it?

He dashed across the street and found a gate in the fence. Locked. Peering through a chink, he saw only darkness beyond. He'd need a better look.

After all he'd been through. It couldn't not be here.

The alley to the left of the construction site was littered with broken glass. The building next door was brick. Some kind of factory? There were no windows on this side, just a loading door. Cassius looked both ways down the alley, then took his chance, running at the chain link fence and leaping. He caught the highest point he could and hung on. Then he climbed, the tips of his Converse pressing into the space between links. At the top, he pulled his bag from his shoulder and let it drop to the far side. The fence wobbled as he swung his legs over. Then he pushed off and dropped.

"What the hell," he muttered, as he worked his way over bits of broken rock. Something had been reduced to rubble here. The old building maybe. He scanned the whole lot. No inn. Just a brand new foundation jutting up from the dirt, smooth and gray.

The streetlights barely cast their light over the high fence, but it was enough to see there was nothing much to look at anyway.

Had Johnny lied to him?

The new concrete foundation was sprawling. Something strange about it though. Usually there were things sticking up, right? Rebar. Plumbing pipes. Something. This was just flat. Weird shape too.

He checked his slip of paper. He couldn't be wrong. Not after everything else he'd been through tonight.

The girl's face came back to him. Her surprise, then her shock. She'd been so young. Too young.

But he couldn't think about her. Not if he wanted to get out. That girl was going to be okay. It wasn't his fault.

None of this had been his fault.

Once he was out of here he could worry about making things right. He felt the added weight of his bag again. Somehow he'd make it right.

But not if he couldn't get free. He checked his watch for the third time and swore.

Where the hell was it?

He kept walking across the seemingly endless concrete.

"Hey!"

The voice was far off at first. He tried to locate it.

"Hey, you!"

There. The figure at the far end of the lot. She was walking fast, arms waving. Looked like she was telling him to move.

The figure flipped on a flashlight and broke into a run.

Cassius pulled at the zipper of his bag and reached a hand inside, feeling for the cold steel of the .45.

But this woman wasn't waving a weapon. Just the light. She was short, black, dressed like a dude.

"You crazy? You aren't supposed to be here!"

Cassius held up his other hand to block the light.

She didn't look like a security guard but she had authority in her voice. She went straight for him and pointed toward the gate in the fence. "Go! Now!"

"Hang on, I'm looking for something," Cassius said.

"A brain injury? Because you already have one if you think you can stand out here and not get flattened. You think I want to scrape your guts off the pool table?"

"What?"

"This," she said, gesturing to the area around them, "is the billiard room. You're about to become a permanent addition to it if you don't clear out. You *are* a guest, right?"

"Guest? Yeah! Yeah, yeah. You mean the inn? The one that jumps around in time? That's what I'm looking for."

"Jumps around," the woman repeated. "Everyone thinks it just shows up, kerpoof! You think that's what all this is? Spontaneous? You know how much work this is? Finding the right time of night? Finding a location and a situation and enough explanations to fend off the bonkers locals? You think that's all this is?"

"No, I just meant—"

"Sure you did. And you thought you could just stroll into the middle of the landing site," she checked her watch, "two minutes before arrival. And you thought somehow you'd just what? Apparate inside? Who are you, Professor Dumbledore?"

"I don't . . . I don't know who that is."

"Sweet mercy," she muttered. "I need a damned raise." She grabbed Cassius's arm and pulled. "Next time you want to commit suicide by building, you just go find a nice tall one and jump off like everyone else, okay? I am not going to be responsible for you. Do you know how many people this inn has crushed on arrival since I've been in charge of relocation?"

"Uh . . ."

"Zero! And you ask why I am in this job and not my predecessors. You ask how their records stack up." She shook her head. "Not zeroes. I'll tell you that."

They reached the edge of the concrete foundation and the fiery woman plucked a key from her pocket. She shoved it into the padlock holding the gate shut and popped it loose. She swung the gate open and gestured to the street. "Now if you'll excuse me, you'll kindly wait on the sidewalk like a normal guest!"

Cassius went through the gate with an extra shove. When he turned around, he was trying to form an apology, but the woman wasn't looking at him anymore. Her eyes were fixed on her watch and her mouth was moving silently, counting.

Cassius looked east. A car's headlights illuminated the night a few blocks down. But when he turned back to the woman, a blast of air blew the words away with the rest of his thoughts.

He blinked the dust from his eyes and squinted as he backed up.

The space behind the woman was now lit. The amber glow of lantern light. Must have been a dozen of them mounted to the white walls. Planter boxes sat in windows. Ivy climbed the walls and roof like the building had stood there a hundred years.

He took two steps back, then three. His mouth hung wide.

Holy shit.

It was just like they'd said.

He smiled, despite himself. Despite everything his night had become. He was getting out. This was going to work.

The woman brushed dust from her short black hair and stuck a thumb toward the steps leading up to the wooden door. She was holding the gate open for him. "Okay. Now it's safe. You coming in or what?"

But Cassius only grinned. Then he turned and ran, back down the street, sneakers slapping the pavement again, dodging around mailboxes and telephone poles. And finally he found a payphone. He dug through his pockets till he came up with a quarter and dropped it in the slot, cradling the handset to his head.

He breathed hard and fast.

Three rings. The line picked up.

"It's here. Just like I said. Come on. It's here!"

CHAPTER 4

Greyson. 2035

"There's a wet spot outside your door," I said, handing the pint glass with the rose in it across the bar to Heavens.

She looked great tonight. Energized. The room glowed a little brighter when she was like this. A woman in her element. Master of her universe.

"What's this? From you?"

"No. Someone else. Found it in the hall outside your door."

She accepted the glass and rose with a shrug and placed it behind the bar. The pub was nearly packed now but she had help. Two other bartenders on tonight.

I spotted Nadia, the woman who had chatted me up earlier at the far end of the bar. She had a bevy of new conversation partners. New blood in the place always stirred up excitement. She didn't bother to look my way.

I was grateful Heavens had taken the time to meet me at the end of the bar with the least amount of noise.

"You okay?" she asked.

"Gotta go see someone tonight. Don't wait for me for the jump."

"Couldn't if I wanted to," Heavens said. "Solena would murder me for even asking. But I know you hate the 1980s, and nobody can blame you for skipping this jump in particular. I won't try to talk you into coming along."

I rubbed the back of my neck. "You know what goes down?"

"Had a basic briefing. It's a complicated situation. But that's what we do here. And I know it was a long time ago for you."

"Fourteen years. Maybe I'll meet up at the next stop. If you still want me around. But I wouldn't blame you if you don't."

She frowned. "I thought we'd have more time to talk, Grey. I've been meaning to apologize."

"For what?"

"What I said the other day. I implied there was a future where you and I were more than friends, and I realized afterwards how irresponsible that was. How much you hate potential paradoxes and the pressure that puts on things to work out a certain way."

"Not a paradox if it happens."

"And I'm not saying I don't believe it will. I'm usually the one who trusts things will work out like they should. But it was still wrong of me to put that on you right now, especially when I knew you weren't ready."

"You say that part as a certainty."

"I am certain, Grey. Unfortunately it's the only thing I'm certain of."

"So you know enough about the future to see signs?"

Heavens put her hands in her back jeans pockets. "I ran into myself this one time. A future version of me. Completely on accident. But she remembered. We were in the same timeline. And she looked happy. And she was with a guy . . . Look, I can't

19

tell you any more. Just know I'm waiting for something specific. I don't know exactly when I'll see it, but when I see it, I'll know."

"Because the future version of yourself told you what to look for."

She put her palms up and shrugged.

"Except it might never happen now. Because you told me about it."

"That's true. I don't know. It's possible I've already diverted us somehow, but it's also still possible I haven't."

"Good God. It's probably best I'm not around. We're confusing the hell out of this. Whatever happened to guy meets girl and takes her to dinner?"

She stared into my eyes without looking away. The air between us was still electric but she was too far to touch.

"I'm sorry, Grey. I gotta get back to work. I'll ping you the coordinates when we land."

"Sure."

She walked away and went back to serving customers. Seemed like every guest of the inn was determined to make the trip with a buzz on.

Didn't blame them.

There were a lot of lighthearted faces in here tonight. No trouble to be found.

But I'd provide enough of that in their near future. Near past. Whatever it was.

This place was getting too complicated.

I walked out and didn't look back.

The Boss was parked in one of the horse stalls in the stable. I pulled the cover off and let the hay dust float around my head. The Mustang's paint gleamed like the surface of a lake at night. Until the dust started to settle onto it. Couldn't have that.

I took the car out of the stable under electric power, but when I got into the drive, I started the gas engine. The horses all looked up from their stalls. Pure jealousy.

"Good evening, Greyson." My onboard AI spoke from the car's speakers.

"We're going for a ride, Waldo."

"On assignment?"

"Something personal."

"Heaven forbid you take a job that pays a fee. By the way, have you seen gas prices lately?"

"We can fill up in a different decade if it makes you happy." I tapped the dash display screen to bring up the nav computer.

"Your heart rate is elevated. Something is bothering you. Does it have to do with the way the inn's next destination coincides with your past?"

"I knew it would happen eventually, but I'd hoped I'd have more time."

"Miss Archer's affection for you appears authentic. Meeting your younger self seems unlikely to change her mind."

"Relationships are finicky, Waldo. Sometimes you only need one chance to make a bad impression."

My concentration had lapsed and I found myself just staring at the car's display screen.

"Shall I map the course for you?" Waldo offered.

"Sure. As soon as I find the coordinates."

I pulled out my phone and located my Timekeeper app. It was a ridiculous name if you thought about it. Time is one thing you're guaranteed never to keep. But they had to call it something. And every time traveler needs a clock. Something personal to track the hours spent in one timeline or another. Past and future become blurry terms when you're bouncing around decades. Finding the progression of others gets tricky too.

The Allied Scientific Coalition of Time Travelers made

personal timekeeping mandatory for travelers as a way to put order to the chaos, and even rule-resistant families like mine had to see the logic of it. In some cases, ASCOTT and the Temporal Crimes Investigation Division made timekeeping part of ongoing monitoring of felons and persons of interest. Persons of interest like seventeen-year-olds who walked into taverns with guns and shot known offenders under suspicious circumstances.

My TCID timekeeping profile was how Captain Black Elk knew when to call me. And I had to admit, the app had uses. I'd skip traced my share of felons with help from the app. It was no use bringing people in before they had even thought to run.

Right now, I needed the app for a different purpose. And the information was in my private contacts, safely secure from the TCID databases. I read the coordinates to Waldo.

"It will take several jumps to make it to the year 2110," Waldo replied.

"Nothing you can't handle, buddy."

"Of course," my AI said. "We've needed a change of scenery. And it's always nice to go home."

CHAPTER 5

Greyson. 2110

I got a lot of stares driving down the road in a late 1960s Mustang in the year 2110. Time Travel wasn't public knowledge yet but everyone knew I was out of my element. A lot like cruising my local decade in a Model T. Luckily, the classics are timeless.

Saint Petersburg was a metropolis in this century. Just when you didn't think Florida could fit any more people, they'd gone and made Tampa Bay a hub for electric power. The eternal sunshine helped. We had solar roads and vertical produce farms. There were zip lanes to ease congestion. Metaspace avatars roamed the streets hocking virtual delights. It was the shiny future we'd been promised. But people still found things to complain about.

I took an elevator fifty stories to reach the penthouse of the building belonging to Piper Travers. When she was in this decade she liked a view, and hers was one of the best in town. When I pressed my finger to the keypad on the door, a picture of me popped up on the security screen. Only it wasn't me. It was the other guy with my fingerprints.

My sister's voice came over the speaker. "You'd better have brought that lovely fiancée of yours!"

"It's the other one," I said. "Sorry to disappoint."

The door unlocked anyway and I walked into the wide-open residence of my older sister. The windows were ten feet tall and bathed the whole place in enough daylight to blind a rainbow.

I found Piper in her kitchen, seated at a granite-topped island you could land a plane on. She had a bottle of wine open and hadn't spilled a single drop on her white linen outfit.

"You look relaxed," I said.

"And you look like you haven't been sleeping."

"Sleep is only for the righteous."

"I wondered why I sleep so well," she said as she slid off her stool to greet me. "Sorry about the mixup at the door. I've been expecting Greyson and Vanessa to stop by. I know you two don't like getting confused for each other."

"Probably bothers him more than me. How is *Professor* Travers?"

"You really care or are you just torturing yourself?"

I took my jacket off and draped it over the back of a sofa. "You know me too well."

"When you show up, it's always for a reason. And it's never to gossip." She gestured to the bottle on the counter. "Can I pour you a glass? It's a Montepulciano. You'll like it."

"Sure."

"Good. You eat yet today?"

I shook my head.

She leaned on the kitchen island. "Hey, Sauron, order up some lunch for Greyson and me, will you?"

"As you wish, My Master," a deep voice said from somewhere overhead

I raised an eyebrow. "You renamed your house AI Sauron?"

24

"Well, if the dark lord of Mordor is waiting on me hand and foot, how cool does that make me?" She grinned.

"I'm sure that will go over great when the singularity happens."

She laughed and it made her freckled nose crinkle. "Don't worry, I'm sure I'll have renamed Sauron by then. He gets a new name about once a month. I think he kind of digs it. You're the one who can't leave the house without one of them. How is yours? Winky? Wilson?"

"Waldo," I said. "And he's fine."

Piper handed me the glass of wine. "Let's go out on the balcony. Not too hot today."

The doors opened automatically as we walked outside. Balcony was a modest description considering it had its own pool, private cantina, and a half dozen deck chairs. We walked to the edge and stared east over the bay. It was breezy and the air smelled like salt.

"You need to keep an eye out," I said at last. "There's a chance you might be in danger."

Piper gave me her full attention. Looked me right in the eye. It was something I'd always liked about her.

"What kind of trouble are *you* in?"

"No more than usual. But Cassius Roseland is out of prison."

She frowned. "I thought Cassius Roseland was dead."

"TCID kept that story up publicly. He was in with some bad people and I think they did it for his protection. Then he decided to play nice for a shorter sentence. Now he's out."

She studied me for a moment longer, then took a sip of her wine. After she swallowed, she said, "Well, good."

"Good?"

"I've been worried about you carrying the weight of that night around all these years. And I'm glad you didn't kill him. You need to move on. Everyone else still thinks he's dead?"

"As far as I know. I wouldn't spread it around that he isn't."

She nodded. And I knew she'd be good to her word. Keeping secrets was another thing Piper had always been good at.

"You can't keep dwelling on what happened all those years ago," she said. "You have to let it go. This makes it easier. Live and let live."

"I don't know. Some things leave a stain."

She narrowed her eyes. "You're talking about something else now. The part you never tell me."

I took a drink and kept my mouth shut.

She rested a hand on my arm. "You never have to tell me what happened, and you know I'm never going to ask, but the fact that I'm standing here says enough. Me, and our other Greyson. I know the life we've had is what it is because it didn't go down a different road. I've never pushed you to tell me what that other road was, but give me credit for knowing something happened."

"I've never once taken you for a fool."

"Good. And the rest of us can help too, Grey. It's not like you're the first duplicate in the family. You remember the story of what happened at Grandpa's funeral? I know you like to keep us at a distance, but you don't always have to go it alone."

"I just came to tell you to be careful. Fourteen years in Rookwood is a long time to be angry. If he's out, he might be looking for payback. I don't know who might be in his sights."

"I can take care of myself."

The wine glass in my hand somehow felt fragile. Like I might lose my grip on it, or break it from holding on too tight. I found a table to set it on. "I should go."

"You don't have to run toward this thing, Grey. If there's going to be trouble, let it come in its own time."

"That's not how I'm going to get more sleep at night."

Piper was still studying me. "Something *else* is bothering you. What's her name?"

26

"No way. We're definitely not going down that rabbit hole. I'll go."

"Okay, fine. Keep your secrets. But don't go yet. Sauron already called out for tacos from that place you like."

"The one on Central?"

"He always gets too much guacamole for the chips. I can't eat it all by myself. You know this." She gave me her best pout.

She had me and she knew it. Older sisters somehow always made the rules. I picked my wine glass back up. But it felt less fragile now. "All right. I'll do it for the guac."

She smiled. "Story of my life."

CHAPTER 6

1984. Cassius. 40 Minutes to Midnight

He checked his Casio again. Nearly eleven thirty. Time was getting short.

They were coming out of the hardware store. He took a deep breath.

It was now or never.

Cassius jaywalked across the street to get on the same side as them. The boy was tall, but lanky. Looked like he needed a few pounds. Cassius remembered those days, scrapping every day in the ring and eating anything he could get his hands on to gain muscle. Wasn't till he was nineteen that he finally packed it on. But to this day Cassius was a lean fighter.

Wasn't all he used to be, he could admit that. If he was, he wouldn't have wound up in Mickey Twitch's pocket. But he was more than a match for a couple of rich white kids.

They were getting ahead of him. He knew these streets though, and when they turned up Fairbanks he knew he could catch them. He sprinted down the alley that ran behind the shoe warehouse and came out the other side on Navarro. There was less foot traffic here too which would be good.

The key was to be fast. He'd flash the gun, grab that watch, and be out of there.

With any luck he'd be gone by the time anyone came looking. Key was to scare these kids bad enough that they didn't immediately send the cops to cut him off. Shit. Would they call regular cops or time cops? Cassius had never met any of those. He frowned. Didn't matter. Anything was better than what Mickey would do if he caught him.

And if he could get his hands on that watch, Mickey never would.

First things his coach ever taught him. Keep moving. Light on your feet. Pop pop. Sting with the jabs. Stay out of the corners. Mickey wanted him in a corner now, but he was going to keep moving. All across time.

The kids were coming down the street, laughing.

The girl was older than he first thought, but still young. Twenty maybe. Tall too, nearly Cassius's height. He could see the resemblance between the pair now. Brother and sister. No doubt about it.

Nobody else around. This was all right. It would work.

He waited. Waited.

Then he stepped from the shadows, gun up.

"Don't fuckin' move!"

They both startled but didn't run.

He waved the gun in their faces. "Don't think. Just do what I say. Watch. I want the watch!"

"What?" The boy had his hands up.

"It's okay," the girl said. "Okay, okay. We have some cash you can have."

"I don't need your damn cash. I want the watch. That one." He pointed to her wrist.

Her hands were up. But she looked over at her brother. "Grey. Grab my shoulder."

"Don't touch nothing!"

"It's okay." The girl was reaching for the watch on her wrist.

But not just a watch. Wait. What was she going to do with it if she touched it? Was this a trick? He realized he didn't know how it really worked.

"We're going to give you whatever you want. No problems. I just need to take it off my wrist."

But the boy's hand went to her shoulder just as her other hand went for the watch.

The gun went off in Cassius's hand without him even thinking about it.

Pop. Pop.

The silence of the next second stretched and stretched.

Then the boy shouted, "Piper!"

Cassius swung the gun toward the kid but the boy wasn't coming at him. He had both arms around his sister as she fell.

Oh shit.

Cassius looked at the smoking gun in his hands.

The girl's eyes were wide, her hands clutching her chest. "I was going to . . . give it . . . ." But then she coughed. Blood trickled from her mouth.

Damn it dammit dammit. Oh fuck. Oh fuck. Cassius backed away a step.

She was on the ground now. Cassius fought the urge to run. Why'd she have to do that? This was supposed to be simple. Not like this.

Oh God.

Move. Move.

No.

He still needed that watch. Focus.

Two steps forward. Her jacket was splayed around her. Which hand was it again? He reached low.

"GET OFF!" the boy screamed. He moved across her body with one hand up, blocking her. Was he going for the watch too?

Cassius swung the pistol and connected with the top of the boy's skull. A hard right cross. The kid flew backward and hit the pavement. The girl fell the rest of the way too without her brother to hold her. Her head hit hard.

Cassius straddled her body and used his free hand to push up the sleeve of her sweater. Blood stains had blossomed on her chest. How did this watch come off?

The boy was dazed, rolling over, reeling in pain.

Cassius fought with the latch. Finally it broke free of her wrist.

The boy was shaking his head, blinking.

"I'm sorry," Cassius said as he straightened. "I'm sorry." He backed up, pocketing the watch.

The boy didn't see him. He crawled back to his sister. "Hang on Piper. I got you. I got you. Don't worry."

But the light in the girl's eyes was dimming, losing consciousness.

Cassius took a step back toward her. Could he do something? No. Fuck. He had to go. He had to go.

He ran.

CHAPTER 7

Greyson. 2110

"I'll find him first. That's the only way this goes our way."

The dull glow of the Boss's instrument panel illuminated my small world. It was still parked in the garage of Piper's building. Warning her of the danger had eased my tension some, but back in the neon phosphorescence of the parking garage, darkness had settled into my mind again. Old memories barely kept at bay.

"The current whereabouts of Cassius Roseland are unavailable," Waldo replied.

"Someone knows where he is. If he's out of Rookwood, he'll need to go somewhere."

"Your sister was of the opinion it would be counterproductive."

"Not everything in the world has to make sense to be the right decision, Waldo. Maybe it's the wrong decision. I just need to know. I want to look into his eyes."

"You believe viewing him in person will give you information you don't currently possess?"

"You can tell a lot about a man from how well he meets your eye. You can see into his soul."

"What do people see when they look into your eyes?"

I glanced at my reflection in the rear view mirror. Then I looked away. "Let's just find him."

Waldo brought up a map of the timestreams in the vicinity of Rookwood Penitentiary on screen.

"No. Black Elk told me he was in a timestream close to his original with a fourteen year gap for his age. Show me timestreams in the nearest proximity to where he left from."

Waldo changed the image. It resembled a web more than a map, but that was the fractal multiverse for you. There were dozens of branches.

"Still a lot of ground to cover," I muttered.

"Your library of temporal anchors will only get us to a few of these locations," Waldo said. "If you would like to chart a course to these other timestreams, you are going to need to supplement our collection."

I swore. Getting around time was never as easy as it sounded. Sure, I had a time traveling car and a chronometer on my wrist. But that would only let me bounce around the timestream I was in. If I wanted to visit alternate branches of the multiverse, I would need something from those places to anchor me to the right time and location. Every smart time traveler had a personal collection of anchors to work with, but personal collections only get you so far.

And I knew the most likely place that would get me what I need. I didn't want to go back there, but it would save me time.

So I shifted the Boss into gear and drove.

Zoran's Hardware sits on the corner of a downtown intersection in a strip of high-rent shops, and has done so for a couple hundred years. Locals rarely give it a passing glance. Occasionally an optimistic tourist wanders in to browse the shelves of oddly categorized junk before the dim lighting and lack of discernible pricing runs them off.

When the rare shopper persists in finding something of interest among the shelves, they make the trek through a maze of clutter to the even darker back counter. There, a wizened woman in a head shawl sips something from a mug that hasn't had a proper wash since the millennium. Upon setting their desired treasure on the counter, the old woman looks up from her dusty cash register and croaks a number in Bosnian.

If the shopper happens to speak Bosnian, they quickly note the price is fifty times the value of the object in question. Any complaint about that price, or a failure to understand Bosnian, causes the old woman to reach across the counter and drag the item away to disappear God-knows-where. She then utters in accented but clear English, "Not for sale."

The tourist usually takes this opportunity to complain further. But the appearance of an enormous and surly man in the doorway behind the old woman typically calms them down. The rowdier and more entitled tourists grumble on the way out, muttering about the scathing review they plan to write, but by the time they are on the sidewalk and find the store's long list of one-star reviews online, they realize most of their complaints have already been colorfully summarized.

Inside Zoran's Hardware Store, the surly man fades into the obscure back room and the old woman sips from her mug, and life goes on.

I'd never met Zoran. Maybe he's dead. Maybe there never was a Zoran.

The old woman's name is Dragana.

Today her shawl was blood-red lace. I didn't bother to ask if she remembered me. When I got close to the counter, she put her hand beneath it and came up with a ledger bound in thick leather. It thudded to the countertop and she waited.

Looked like she did remember.

I took the slip of paper I'd written my coordinates on and slid it to her. Her wrinkled hand plucked it from the surface of the glass and she studied the alpha-numerical codes.

"Can you get me to these timestreams?" I asked. "Vicinity of May, 1998."

She grunted.

As she opened the huge tome in front of her, I considered informing her of the advent of computers. Excel spreadsheets. I'm sure there was an app somewhere that could handle this job on a phone. But Dragana didn't look like a woman who made a lot of calls. The doorway to the back room was dark today and obstructed by cardboard boxes. If anyone was back there, I couldn't hear them.

Dragana finally located what she was looking for in the ledger and slid off her stool. She shuffled around the counter and into the maze. I followed.

When she found the shelf she was looking for, she stooped and reached into the darkness, squinting. A few things clattered. Then she stood again, a tarnished door knocker in her hand. She turned it over and checked the numbers engraved in the back. She repeated this process several more times, handing me some of the items and never once referring to the slip of paper I'd given her. Then she grunted again and shuffled her way back to the counter.

I had a wad of cash out by the time she regained her place at the register. She eyed my hand.

"Cronus only."

"When did you stop taking dollars?"

She shrugged. "Bad economy."

I frowned and put my local currency away, then opened my

jacket and unzipped the hidden pocket inside. This wad of bills was thinner and the denominations were smaller.

"Fifty," she said. "Each."

I didn't know the current exchange rates but I knew this pile of rusty trinkets was costing me close to a grand apiece. I also knew not to complain. I counted out the bills. "I'll need imagery."

Dragana sighed. Then she dinged the silver bell on the counter. A light turned on in the back and the big dude appeared. She said something in Bosnian. He disappeared again. Dragana and I stared at each other. After a minute, the big guy was back. He had a stack of bug-eaten manilla envelopes. He passed them to Dragana and she opened each. There were photos inside. She rifled through the stack, checking the codes on the back, finally plucking several photos out. She stared at me.

I gave her the money. She proceeded to check it with a hand scanner.

Apparently modern technology was acceptable when it came to catching temporal counterfeiters.

She bent to her ledger with a pen and scratched out a line from the row of numbers, repeating the task for each item she'd given me. Then she turned the ledger around and offered me the pen. "You sign here." I did. Then the pen went back into its tin with a clink and the ledger slammed shut. She handed me the photos.

"Always a pleasure," I said. I studied the pile of anchors. "Got a bag?"

"You bring own bag to Zoran's," she said. "Better for environment."

I sighed and shoved the door knocker into my back pants pocket, then loaded the rest of the items into my jacket pockets.

"I need some information too. If I give you the date and time, can you tell me which transactions you did that day?"

"Why would I?"

I got my now slimmer wad of cronus back out.

She considered me. "Business or personal?"

"Don't worry about it." I told her the date.

She shuffled over to a bookshelf and located another of the leather-bound tomes, hefting it slowly and slamming it down on the counter with another thud. "Nineteen-eighty-four." She swatted at the dust that swirled up toward her face, then set to work rifling through pages.

When she found the date and time she was looking for, she looked up. "Name?"

"Piper Travers."

Her finger went down the line and paused. "Here." She turned the book around and showed me the entry. "Three anchors."

I recognized my sister's neat signature.

"These other entries before it were the same day?"

She nodded.

The entry ahead of Piper's listed a ticket sale for the Rose 'n Bridge tavern and the rental of a portable gravitizer.

I frowned. Cassius Roseland had only left initials. No contact info.

But he'd bought two tickets.

I tossed my remaining bills on the counter and walked out.

CHAPTER 8

Cassius. 1984. One hour till midnight.

Place didn't look like no hardware store he had ever heard of. Nothing in here was going to help you plug a leak or fix a fence. But this was the place Johnny had always talked about. The place time travelers did their business.

Cassius felt the weight of his duffel bag. Extra heavy now.

An electric bell chimed when he got past the linoleum and the door mats. The place smelled like rust and dust. Something else too. Incense? Candles? Maybe it was old people.

The air was thick, like it hadn't been circulated in a long time.

The floor was carpeted once you got past the entrance. Who carpeted a hardware store? But the place was still open. That was something.

His Casio said 10:59 pm.

He tried to look casual, like maybe he was just a shopper. But the old woman at the back counter kept her eyes on him just the same. Finally he approached.

"Sup," he offered.

She had a head shawl on. One of those church lady kind. But she didn't look like a church lady.

"I hear this is the place I can get a ticket to that tavern. The one that goes through time."

The old woman sized him up. Then she spit some tobacco juice through a gap in her teeth into a can.

Nasty.

But he'd been around worse.

"How many tickets?" she said.

"Two. Need two tickets."

The woman reached below her and hoisted a thick ledger up to the countertop. "Two tickets, standard tour, five hundred. Reservation name?"

"Uh. Johnny McKee."

"I'll need some ID."

He was worried about that. Cassius took out Johnny's wallet and fished out the driver's license. Sometimes if you put your finger over the photo and held it up, people wouldn't look too close.

She looked up and studied him. Held out a hand.

Damn it. He handed over the ID.

She glanced at it, then back up at him.

He looked nothing like Johnny. He knew it, she knew it.

He pulled the strange multi-colored bills from the extra fold of the wallet and held them ready.

"This reservation is only for one."

"I got the money for two though. My friend sent me to pick it up." He held the shiny bills out, easy for her to reach. "I got the five hundred right here. Don't need no extra room or nothing, just going to share. It's cool."

She was looking right through him. Like Superman or something.

After what felt like an eternity, she reached for the bills.

"I give you tickets, but if they no let you in, not my fault, understand?"

"That's all right. Just give me the tickets. We'll sort it out."

"Both persons time travel before?" she croaked.

"Nah, that's the other thing I got to talk to you about. I had that treatment, you know. The one with the blue juice makes your mouth all tingly and that box that zaps you up and gets you ready to go. But my friend ain't had that yet and we need it done quick."

Her eyelids only seemed like they went part way up now. Maybe she was tired.

"You got a way to help with that?" Cassius pressed.

The old woman grunted. "Gravitite treatment of person is expensive. Off-record, more expensive. Fast and off-record?" She left the question hanging in the air. But she hadn't put the ledger away.

There was no more of the iridescent cash in the wallet. But Cassius wasn't out of moves. He pulled his duffel bag around to the front of his body and unzipped it. The old woman watched every movement. It took some doing, but he got the bar out and slid it across the countertop.

It sat there gleaming like the day it was minted. Four hundred ounces of pure gold.

Cassius didn't know the exact exchange rate, but he knew they were both looking at over a hundred grand in 1984 dollars.

And it would be worth more to a time traveler.

She looked from him to the bar and back again. Then she shouted. "Nikola!"

Cassius waited.

A shadow loomed in the back doorway and one of the biggest whitest dudes he'd ever seen stepped through. Pale like a ghost. Eyes two different colors. Cassius had his hand on the strap of his bag but wished he'd kept it inside with the .45. If this guy was about to take what was his, he'd have a hard time stopping him, even with the gun.

The old woman spoke to the guy in a language Cassius didn't understand. Coulda been saying anything. Grab him. Kill him. Smash him with this gold brick.

But the big pale dude just nodded and went back through the doorway he'd come from.

The old woman made a note in her ledger. She studied the gold bar some more, then went to a cash register and started counting out some of those funky bills. By the time she was done counting, the big guy was back with a small, hard-sided black case. He set it on the counter and opened it. It had a bottle of that blue juice in it. The rest of the contraption looked used. Some kind of sack and some poles that linked together and a power cord and some shit Cassius couldn't even name.

"Is dangerous if you don't know what you are doing," the old woman said. "Still dangerous if you do."

"Look, I don't got a lot of choices, right? It come with some kind of instructions?"

She said something else to the big dude and he replied. Then he picked up the box in the case with the power cord attached and gestured to a user manual stuck underneath.

Cassius hoped it was in English.

The old woman handed him a slim stack of bills. "This is rental. You give back, I return deposit."

"Cool. Right on," Cassius said. He closed the lid on the contraption and worked on stuffing it into his duffel bag. She nodded to the big guy and he scooped up the gold bar.

"Sign for gravitizer here. Tickets here." The old woman had turned the ledger around and was offering him a pen.

Cassius took the pen and bent over the ledger. Should he lie about who he was? He couldn't think of any better names so he just scribbled CR.

"You want to be added to email list?" the old woman asked.

"What's a email?"

She turned the ledger back around. "I put no."

The bell at the front of the store dinged.

Cassius glanced behind him but couldn't see past the shelves.

The voices were youthful. A girl and a guy.

Cassius finished zipping his bag and made for the door, using a different aisle than the new customers. Fewer people saw him here the better. But he paused when they passed, catching a glimpse through the shelves as they went by. He stopped to watch as they approached the counter.

The only time travelers Cassius had ever met were Johnny and Mickey and a few of the other tough guys that hung around Mickey.

These two walking in weren't anything like Mickey's crew. It wasn't just that they were young, or tall, you could just tell by the way they walked and the way they dressed that they were different. Clothes were clothes and hairstyles were just hair, but there was something fresh about them. Other.

Like they were movie stars and the rest of the world was just scenery.

The old lady at the counter was standing a little straighter too. Paying attention in a way he hadn't noticed was missing when she was talking to him.

"You look for something special today?" she asked.

"We like special," the girl said. "You have anything new for us?" She had a confident way of speaking. Long brown hair. Maybe an athlete.

The trio lapsed into a conversation that was beyond Cassius's ability to follow. All about "anchor points" and names of places he'd never heard of. The old woman kept looking at the girl's left wrist and the elaborate watch she was wearing.

"You willing to sell that? I give you good money. Five million US."

Cassius blinked. She was going to give the girl five million dollars for her watch? He looked at it again. And then he saw that it wasn't just a watch.

The girl's laugh was honest. "I'd be a fool to ever sell this kind of freedom. And we'd never get home. We just came for anchors."

"I give you ten million," the old woman pressed.

It was a personal time machine. Had to be.

Cassius had only ever heard rumors. Getting the right particle treatment to become a time traveler was one thing. Having your own way to get around was something else entirely. None of the guys hanging around Mickey Twitch had anything and Mickey himself only let them use his gateway to New York. It went to specific places but not many. That's why Cassius had a chance to outrun him if he could get aboard that crazy inn. But imagine if he had his own time machine watch. Mickey would never find him.

Cassius looked at these two kids and their casual ease and tried to imagine what life must feel like for them. A whole universe at their fingertips. A multiverse of freedom.

And in that moment he knew what he had to do.

He backed slowly down the aisle, then ran to the door, the chime dinging as he fled outdoors.

CHAPTER 9

Greyson. June, 1998. Timestream N7X5

He was a furniture company manager this time. It was the fifth timestream I'd tried and I already knew he wasn't the right guy.

"You're confident this isn't the Cassius Roseland we're looking for," Waldo said.

We were parked across from the store's loading bays, watching the Cassius Roseland from this time chat with coworkers as they entered the building.

"The one from my time broke his nose the night he shot my sister. Look how straight this guy's nose is. It's like he was never even a fighter. And that's not the look of a dude who just got out of prison."

The Cassius across the street was wearing a white polo shirt with a name badge. Guys were listening to him like they'd been doing it all their lives. This wasn't some new manager who just showed up last week.

People take for granted what it feels like to be a native of a time. Linears never have a choice. But for time travelers, adjusting to a new decade is harder than it looks. Cassius went to prison in 1984 and was dropped back into linear time in 1998. Rookwood might have shown an occasional episode of Seinfeld, but I doubted he felt at home in this time yet. The guy out the window was smiling, laughing, clearly well-liked. He'd done something right in his life. Starting with never shooting my sister.

I was looking for a killer.

"Something doesn't add up here," I muttered. "Every timestream we've visited so far already has a Cassius. There's no way our guy would fit in unless they replaced him. That's not something TCID usually does."

"It could be a timestream where the existing Cassius is deceased," Waldo offered.

"Could be. Maybe we filter by searching for death certificates prior to 1998."

Waldo immediately set to searching available databases.

But it still bothered me.

Something wasn't right and my gut wouldn't let it go.

I watched this oblivious Cassius go about his business out the window and stewed on it awhile longer.

When it finally hit me, I smacked my palm to my forehead. "God, I'm blind."

"Do you require medical attention?" Waldo asked.

"Possibly. Just to get my head out of my ass. We're looking in the wrong place. Black Elk *lied*."

"You're suggesting Captain Black Elk deliberately deceived you?"

"He told me Cassius was in an alternate timestream because he knew I'd go *looking* and would be on a wild goose chase. I'm betting that means they put Cassius back in the one place he said he wouldn't be—his original timestream."

"Perhaps you've become predictable."

"This isn't Black Elk's first rodeo. I don't blame him for misleading me."

"Have you then learned your lesson and are ready to return home chastised?"

"Fat chance."

I got out of the car.

"Is this a good—" Waldo began. But I hit the control on my phone and shut him off.

Walking across the street I caught little attention, but as I approached the gaggle of workers around their boss, more eyes turned my direction. Cassius Roseland turned my way too. The man in charge.

"Hey," I said. "You got a minute?"

"Something I can help you with?"

"Looking for some information."

He turned to one of his employees. "Help him out will you? I need to get back to the office."

The woman faced me obligingly.

"Has to be you," I said, moving past her.

The woman shrugged to her boss.

He frowned, but hid it quickly, checking his watch. "Sure. How can I help you?"

"You seem happy here. Well-adjusted. You have any reasons why your life is so great?"

The question took him aback. "You're asking why I seem . . . happy? Does this have to do with a job?"

"No. Has to do with you."

A few of his employees were still paying attention, but Cassius waved them away. "You all can get back to it. We'll rally up again at the end of the day." The workers slowly dispersed, a few giving me curious glances.

"So, found God, maybe?" I asked. "Something different in your childhood?"

He studied me. "You searching for some answers, buddy? That what this is?"

"Searching. Sure."

"Can't say I take the credit for how my life has turned out. I work hard, do what I can to help others. Have a good wife. Good family."

"Your parents alive?"

His face darkened. "They aren't, actually. Mom died when I was young. I was a foster kid. But I got a second chance. Some opportunities I took advantage of. You lose someone?"

I stared into his eyes. Sincere eyes. There was empathy there.

"Yeah. Lost someone close. Killed by a bad man."

"Sorry to hear that."

"You ever feel like *you're* a bad man?"

He put his hands in his pockets. "We all have the seeds in us, don't we? Good and bad. It's about the ones you chose to let grow."

"Your foster parents the ones who gave you that second chance?"

"Yes, they did. I know we don't all get that lucky though. That's why I'm paying it back. Got two kids of my own at home right now. Trying to give them a second chance too."

"What's the name of the foster care? One you grew up in."

He told me.

I crossed my arms. "You ever fight?"

"I'm sorry?"

"Ever thrown a punch? Hit a guy in the face?

He tensed.

"Wanna hit me?"

He stared. "Look, man. Seems like you have some things to work out. I hear you. Life deals a tough hand some days. But every day is a new day. New chance. You wake up, you take it."

"I've never believed in second chances."

He checked his watch again, gave me another sizing up. "Can't be all bad." He glanced behind me. "Got yourself a cool car, at least." Two steps back, then three. "Best of luck to you, buddy. Hope you find what you're looking for."

I watched him walk all the way into the furniture warehouse before I went back to the car.

CHAPTER 10

Cassius. 1984. Two hours till midnight.

It was so much gold.

He stared into the trunk of the Oldsmobile and gawped at it.

Could he just leave it somewhere? Let Mickey find it whenever?

When Johnny had told him what they'd be doing tonight, he knew it would be heavy. But nobody really expected to see a half ton of gold in the flesh. Thirty-eight bars they'd pulled from that casket. Nineteen-eighty-four prices meant just one of these bars could go for 150K. But what blew his mind was when Johnny had said in only forty years they'd be worth 750K each.

All the people in the future must be crazy rich. That's all he knew.

Johnny said they had electric cars that drove themselves, and anything you wanted just showed up at your house because everybody shopped with computers that could talk to you. Only it was all done on your telephone. He said nobody had to carry a boombox for music and you got any movie you wanted right in your house on a TV as big as your wall. Johnny said in the future nobody gave a shit if you were queer, and the country already had a black president and a woman one and even made it so you could smoke reefer in your house and not get busted. Nobody even died of AIDS anymore.

That future sounded all right.

But Cassius knew he'd never see any kind of future if he didn't get the hell away from Mickey Twitch.

Mickey was going to come for his gold and he'd think nothing about breaking Cassius's fingers and knees to get it. Maybe fry him up with a car battery like they did in the movies.

He checked his Casio.

Where the hell do you do put an Olds Cutlass full of gold bars so time travelers can't find it?

Probably stupid to even try.

It was impossible to hide it forever. And it had to be somewhere Cassius could get to it again if he needed it. Like if Mickey had a guy with a hammer breaking his knees.

Mickey had all the advantages, but Cassius did know this neighborhood. He knew where the cops walked, knew where the kids played, where the old people hung out. More he thought about it, he also knew a blind man named Jimmy with a big backyard and an old car a lot like this one sitting in the tall grass under a tarp. Pretty sure that old car still ran too, on account of he'd seen the old man's delinquent grandkid use it to try to pick up chicks when he came to visit last summer.

This time on a weeknight, Jimmy was asleep.

Shit. That just might work.

The fence never locked right. Cassius had mowed Jimmy's yard a couple times when he was a teenager and had hauled the mower in the same way he was getting in tonight. Just had to whack that latch real hard and it'd pop loose. Did a bad job of mowing back then but Jimmy never cared. Not like he could see it anyway. Looked like nobody had mowed in a while now. Maybe if he ever came back he'd mow it for him again. Do a real nice job.

Gate swung open on stiff hinges. Didn't squeak too much though. He was grateful for that. Windows were mostly dark except for the room with the TV. That one still flickered but it didn't mean anything.

The tarp had a bunch of bird shit and leaves all over it. Dark back here too, only light coming from a bare bulb on the side porch Jimmy probably didn't know was on. He'd tell him when he came back for the car, save the guy some on his electric bill.

Hard to say when he'd be back. As soon as the heat was off with Mickey, but how long would that take? Judging by the state of the car, it had been sitting for months. A few more likely wouldn't hurt anything. But he'd be back sooner if he could.

He laid the tarp in the grass and got the driver door open by putting an arm through the wind wing and rolling the window down. Dome light came on good and bright. That was a good sign. He was set to fight with the column and hotwire it but he took a look around first. Visors, floor mats, glove box.

A little magnetic key box was hidden under the left rear fender. How about that.

Three pumps on the accelerator and that old car came right to life. God bless that delinquent kid. Hope juvie was treating him all right.

It was short work getting the car backed out and pulling the Olds into the same spot. Sat a little lower with all that weight in it, but not by much.

He stashed the key to the Olds in the magnetic key box and stuck it in the same place it had been on the other car. If Jimmy came out to run this engine, would he tell the difference? Probably, but it couldn't hurt to hope it might fool him.

Before he pulled the tarp over the Olds, he got his bag out of the back and retrieved his change of clothes. He stripped right there in the high grass and stuffed his dirty things in a ball behind the driver's seat. He took one last look at the gold stacked on the floor under there. Hard not to just stare at it, even in this light.

Pity Jimmy was never going to see the treasure hiding in his own backyard. Assuming Cassius could pull this off.

Millions in gold bars.

He took one for the road.

CHAPTER 11

Greyson. 1998.

I was sitting at a 24-hour diner having a waffle when I remembered to turn Waldo back on. The tone chimed in my ear as he came online. I had time to chew two more bites before he got around to speaking.

"My settings say I've been offline for several hours. Did your conversation with Cassius not go well?"

"Went fine. Not the guy we're looking for, obviously. Didn't seem violent. Even offered him a chance to punch me just to see how he'd react."

"That's an odd request, even for you."

"Wanted to know if he secretly wanted to."

"Is there a science to this methodology I am unaware of?"

"Beats me. Didn't look like he wanted to hit me though. I'll give him that. A lot of guys at least think about it."

"Shocking."

It started to rain outside. Afternoon thunderstorm moving in off the gulf.

"How many people have you asked to hit you?" Waldo asked.

"I've lost track." I took another bite of waffle.

Waldo waited till a server with a polka-dot scrunchy in her hair had finished refilling my coffee before he spoke again. "I've noticed you have turned me off several times lately. It leaves gaps in my ability to assist you."

"Sometimes I don't need your help."

"Yet, it is my job to help you. There are times when you may not be conscious of the need."

"There are some things I keep private, Waldo. Even from you."

"It has made me aware that I also have a deficiency of information regarding the years prior to my activation."

"That's what history books are for."

"I meant your personal history."

"You know what you need to, buddy."

"Except that may not be accurate if events in your past affect decisions in your present."

"If there is something you want to know, ask me. If I want to tell you, I will. If not, I won't."

"Okay. This isn't a case," Waldo said. "You haven't been hired to find Cassius Roseland. Why do you continue to investigate him?"

"I told you. I need to look him in the eyes and know what he's capable of."

"You want to predict the future regarding his actions."

"We all try to predict the future, Waldo. We avoid risks, take precautions, try to influence the world in our favor. No one wants to walk blindly into the future. Shit happens beyond the scope of our ability to predict it, but we prepare for that too. It's why insurance companies are so loaded. In this case, I want a different kind of security."

"You don't believe Cassius Roseland is capable of change."

"The man killed my sister."

"So he will always remain your enemy?"

"We have bad blood between us. I don't know anything can wash that clean."

"If the Cassius Roseland in this timeline had hit you, what would you have done?"

"I'd have hit him back."

"And that would have been satisfying?"

"Maybe." I pushed my plate away.

I paid my bill at the register by the door, and shrugged into my jacket. The Boss was parked close but it was still raining. Puddles were growing around the car. I put my collar up and walked out anyway.

By the time I made it to the car and closed the door, my hair was soaked.

I shivered.

"Waldo. Let's go somewhere dry."

A jump location popped up on the nav computer.

I shifted into gear and rolled out, watching the slick road vanish beneath the car. When we reached the jump point, I deployed the car's spacial grounding rod and it sparked off the pavement. I activated the jump trigger in the stick shift and the storm clouds were instantly replaced by a starry sky.

I checked my hair. Better. We'd left most of the water we'd acquired behind. I rolled the windows down. "Waldo, what's the gravitite concentration on the Boss these days?"

"Exterior gravitite to mass ratio is nominal and the vehicle remains temporally permeable."

I opened the center console and removed a small cylindrical item with a test button on it. I aimed the open end of the tube at my left hand and pressed the button. The light flashed red and a number popped up on the car's display screen. It was a big number.

"Your personal gravitite to mass ratio is nearing maximum advisable levels and is temporally impermeable."

"At least I retained my waffle then," I said and put away the test device.

The temporally unstable particles that allowed time travel were a gift and a curse. They allowed objects to jump through decades but they also somehow multiplied over time. Being born a time traveler meant the concentration of particles in my body was more than double that of a newly infused traveler. Handy for not losing your lunch every time you jumped, since the particles formed a denser net, but concentration levels were something to monitor. There were rumors floating around that generations of time travelers procreating together might lead to children so temporally unstable they'd be incapable of existing in one reality.

Good thing I wasn't doing any procreating.

I had an unbidden flash of green eyes and golden hair.

And sparks.

"Hey Waldo. Where's the Rose 'n Bridge right now?"

But then I remembered.

"The Rose 'N Bridge Inn and Tavern is scheduled to be in March, 1984 per your current orientation."

I'd already been there. Wonder how Heavens felt seeing the seventeen-year-old version of me in a shootout tonight.

"Would you like me to plot a course to intercept the inn?" Waldo asked.

I rested my hands on the steering wheel and sighed. "Not till I've seen this through. We're going back to Cassius's original timeline in nineteen-ninety-eight. I don't expect he'll be hard to find. I have a good idea where to look."

Waldo reset the navigation computer for destinations in the target timeline.

"It will be nice to have this situation resolved so that we can get back to working cases that pay," he said.

"Agreed. But first let's go see if the past is going to stay in the past."

I hit the accelerator and we raced into the night.

CHAPTER 12

Cassius. 1984. An hour and a half till midnight.

They were going to die. That's all Cassius knew.

His sister was crying on the floor in the kitchen. He'd heard her tell the story twice now. The knife she'd kept around ever since they were kids was on the living room floor.

But it hadn't protected her. Not really.

Johnny "Fastball" McKee was dead on the carpet, but they were dead now too. It was just a matter of time. Mickey Twitch wouldn't care that their mother had been beaten to death by some john when they were kids. He wouldn't care that his sister had only been crashing on his couch tonight because she couldn't stand another night in that shithole home they'd placed her in.

She'd just reacted. Kitchen knife under the pillow like always. Startled awake. Johnny leaning over and scaring the hell out of her.

He'd warned him not to wake her. Idiot would be alive if he'd listened. And dead for what? Just to leer at a sixteen-year-old sleeping? Not that he was surprised. Johnny hollered and grabbed at any girl in his vicinity. Everyone knew it. But that didn't help them now. Not with Mickey.

Cassius walked to the window and looked out. The Oldsmobile was still there, no one the wiser. But this was a time bomb. Someone might have heard her shout.

"Get your things. We're leaving," he said.

His sister was frozen to the floor next to the refrigerator. He rushed to the closet and pulled down his old backpack. He threw it at her. "Only what you need. And get that blood off your face. Now."

She got slowly to her feet.

Cassius took another look at Johnny. God that was a lot of blood. She'd caught an artery. Anywhere else and he'd have been alive. Pissed, but alive.

He got closer, rolled Johnny to the side enough to fish his wallet from his back pocket. It took several tugs to get it loose.

He checked inside and found it only had thirty bucks in cash in it, but when he pried open the second fold, he found another five hundred in that strange currency the time travelers used. It shimmered weird. He put the whole wallet in his pocket.

His pants were still covered in dirt from digging. It was no good. They couldn't draw attention to themselves. He pulled a change of clothes from his dresser and stuffed it in a bag.

Ten minutes later they were climbing into the car. He tossed his sister's bag into the back seat and threw his own bag in too. He checked the area. He stared into the darkness down each side of the street but saw nothing out of place. That black Mustang he'd seen earlier was gone. He climbed behind the wheel.

"Where are we going, Cass?" Her voice trembled.

"Gotta buy us some time."

Even saying it out loud sounded weak. Mickey Twitch and his men were time travelers. Where could Cassius hope to hide? But then he remembered what Johnny had said near the gravesite. That tavern. The one that jumped all around. He fished in his pockets and took out Johnny's wallet. That card was still there. Was it possible? An address was listed on the back. He'd said it was showing up tonight. Midnight.

Maybe. Just maybe.

He shifted into gear and drove, slow with how heavy the car was, eyes flicking to the rear view mirror like clockwork.

They weren't dead yet. Just needed a ticket out. For both of them. Only one place in town he knew he could get what he needed. He'd never been but he knew where it was. Close enough he might still make it.

They stopped at the late-night gas station at the edge of the neighborhood. Well-lit. He'd been in here before. The old Koreans that ran the place were harmless. The woman had once let him pay her later on a day he forgot his wallet. Not many people still did that in these days. He climbed out and memorized the number on the payphone.

His sister followed.

He gestured to a low wall that surrounded a planter. "You're going to wait right here."

"I'm going with you."

"No you ain't. But I'll come back, or I'll call this phone right here once I know it's safe. I'm not back in an hour or two, then there's trouble. Then you run."

"I want to come with you."

"Don't worry. I'm coming back, or I'll call you to say where to meet me." He gave her the thirty dollars cash from Johnny's wallet and another ten from his own. "This is cab fare to meet up. And get some food. There's a place we can go that I think is a way out for us, but I gotta check it out first." He walked to the passenger side of the car.

She was shivering on the sidewalk. Wasn't even that cold out.

He paused, watching her. Something in him wanted to go

back. Hold her till she stopped trembling. But if he did, it was going to be even harder for her to let go.

This was going to work out. He'd call her as soon as he could and she'd be safer without him till then.

He only looked back once as he drove away. She was still standing there shivering.

CHAPTER 13

Cassius. 1984. Two hours till midnight.

"I'm gonna shower in your apartment. You watch the car," Johnny said.

"Hold up," Cassius replied. "Why aren't we going to your place?"

"We're late already. Micky's going to be missing his shit. He don't see us back soon, he'll send guys out looking."

"If he wanted it faster, he shoulda sent them to help dig."

Johnny put a hand out. "Give me your house key. I'll clean up, then we switch."

Cassius put his hand in his pocket. "Don't wake up my sister. She's probably sleeping and you'd scare the hell out of her if you do."

"I'm a damn ninja," Johnny said. He opened the glove box and pulled his pistol out. He handed the .45 to Cassius grip-first. "You see *anybody* get close to this car, you shoot their asses, you get me? Especially in this neighborhood."

"Where you live so much better?"

Johnny grinned as he climbed out of the car. He pushed the

door closed quietly. "After tonight, you and me are both moving up." He patted the windowsill and pointed at Cassius before he walked away.

Cassius watched him work his way to the stairs at the far end of the apartment block then start up. Didn't move like a ninja. Practically limping. "Damned sure better be quiet," he muttered. He felt the weight of the gun in his hands. Always so much heavier than they looked in the movies. He checked the magazine. It was only half full. Five shots. He found a few loose rounds in the glove box and loaded them in the magazine.

He checked the mirrors. Most of the lights in the neighborhood were out. His Casio read 9:45 pm. He reached under the seat. Still there.

Loading the car had taken longer than they'd figured. Had to move the bars around the Olds so the back suspension would hold. All the weight in the trunk had made the car look ridiculous, not to mention the muffler was scraping the asphalt. Had to reposition a bunch of bars under their seats. Johnny had even held a couple in his lap. One was in the seat now. Foolish. Cassius scooped it up with both hands and put it in the glove box. He let out a laugh. He couldn't help it.

He was sitting on millions of dollars worth of gold bullion.

In an Oldsmobile Cutlass.

It was pure insanity. And the guys he was working for could pull this kind of stunt whenever they needed to.

The money didn't belong to Mickey Twitch any more than it belonged to him or Johnny. He knew it would all be moved around. New York probably. He wouldn't see any of it. But if he did a good job, showed he could be trusted, then he'd be part of the crew.

They'd already given him the treatments. Hadn't gone anywhere yet, but they locked him in that crazy machine, made him drink the strange blue liquid. He could still feel the way it made his face tingle. Like licking a battery. Gravitite particles they'd called it. Time travel juice. His blood was full of it now.

Once they had the shipment to Mickey Twitch, rumor was they'd all be going to New York. But not the New York he knew. New York a few years back, January 1980 when the gold prices peaked. It would get sold then and the money would buy more gold some other time. Cheaper gold. These guys would bury it again most likely. Some other stiff's casket perhaps. It would hide there till the prices were up again. All legal. Well, mostly.

He checked the rear view mirror again. There was an old car in front of that abandoned crack house. Had it been there all day? Yeah, probably. He checked the side view. Looked like maybe someone was in it.

Shit.

Maybe it was one of Mickey's other guys.

That would make sense. Maybe they were extra protection. Insurance. Maybe Johnny had called them. Car was blacker than black. Hard to even see it back there. Mustang maybe?

He fidgeted with the gun some more. Where the hell was Johnny?

He leaned over and looked out the passenger window. A light was on in the apartment. How long could it take to shower off? Cassius checked out the rear window again. Damn it.

Hurry up, Johnny.

His Casio read 10:05 when Cassius finally opened the car door and stood. The apartment light was still on. But no Johnny. Five more minutes. He'd give him five minutes.

At 10:09 he locked the car doors and tucked the .45 into the waistband of his jeans. He'd be able to see the car from the balcony of the apartment. If someone ran up and tried to jack the car, he'd shoot and scare them off. He only needed to make it up and open the apartment door. Johnny had to be done soon.

Was the guy in the Mustang still there? He couldn't tell. If it was one of Mickey's guys, why not identify himself?

Cassius tried to look casual. Why shouldn't he be? It was his place. He walked this walk every day. But he didn't leave millions in gold bars unattended every day.

The walk up the stairs blocked the car from view but only for a few seconds. He sprinted up the second set of stairs onto the upper floor balcony and breathed easier once he saw the car still there.

Just a few more yards.

He reached the door to his apartment and felt around for his key. He'd given it to Johnny.

He tried the doorknob and it opened.

The shriek almost made him drop the gun.

Shit.

He fumbled it and pushed the door open the rest of the way.

"Cass? Oh God."

His younger sister rushed to him. She was in the sweatpants and tank top she'd had on earlier. But it was stained now. Flecked with blood?

"What the hell—" he said. But she was grabbing his arm, pulling him toward the living room. When she reached the archway and pointed, he could already feel the sickness rising in his gut. He flicked on the light.

Johnny Fastball McKee was on the floor next to the couch. The reddening carpet was a halo of blood. He had one hand held to a gash in his throat, but he was staring open-eyed at the ceiling.

CHAPTER 14

Greyson. May, 1998.

"This is certainly ill-advised," Waldo said.

I was sitting on the fender of the Boss with a mostly empty coffee cup in my hand. The boxing gym across the street was a converted warehouse that sat between a junkyard and a motorcycle repair shop. This wasn't a gym for lycra and Jazzercise. No Tae Bo either.

"Has to be done," I said. "I need to know where we stand."

I left the coffee cup on top of the car and walked across the street. I pulled off my shades and earpiece and stuffed them in my pocket. Waldo could sit this out.

A guy coming out of the place gave me a hard look but held the door with his foot.

I'd taken my share of punches on the street, but walking into this place I was out of my element. I was in jeans for one, and being over thirty practically made me a senior citizen. Guys I passed were young and still hungry. Ready to fight the world.

There were multiple boxing rings inside. Speed bags, weight benches. A lot of York barbells and zero smoothie bars.

Only a dozen or so guys were in at this time of the morning but they were working out hard.

Big grizzled dude near a water cooler looked like a coach. He sized me up as I walked in, crossing his arms and presenting himself as a barricade. He had a tattoo on his left wrist of a watch face with no hands. Some dot patterns and the spider web on his elbow looked to be acquired in prison too.

"What's your business, brother?" His long hair made him look like he could be a TV wrestler.

"I'm looking for Cassius Roseland."

"Never heard of him."

I reached into my pocket and extracted a photograph. Cassius's mugshot.

Big guy looked at it. "Doesn't go by Cassius. Name's CJ here. He expecting you?"

"Maybe."

"Maybe not?"

"Just need to have a few words with him."

He studied me some more. "So you know, we don't tolerate any guns, knives, drugs, booze, or hate in here. You got a score to settle, you do it in the ring."

"I'm unarmed and sober. That's the best I can offer."

"It's a start." He uncrossed his arms and gestured toward the back. "You'll find CJ on the heavy bags. Been doing some good work back there."

"Thanks."

"Go in peace, brother."

I walked between two of the boxing rings to get to the back. A pair of fighters were sparring in one, drilling each other, all jabs and hooks. A sign on the wall behind them had a Muhammed Ali quote: *You don't lose when you get knocked down. You lose when you stay down.*

The heavy bags were around a corner in another room and I

heard the thumping first. When I finally had them in view it was just Cassius, shirt off, hands wrapped, hitting.

Smelled like sweat in there. Ceiling was lower, lights dimmer.

Thump thump.

Thump thump thump.

Jab, jab, right cross, left hook.

Then he saw me.

His hands were still up, fists clenched. His eyes widened and we stared at each other.

Fourteen years had aged him plenty but it might as well have been 1984 again.

His hands finally dropped to his sides and he exhaled.

I realized I'd been holding my breath too.

"Figured you'd find me one day," he said. "Didn't expect it this quick."

Prison hadn't diminished his fitness any. He stood dripping, only slightly thicker in the gut than I remembered. A man approaching middle-age but still a weapon.

He unwrapped his left wrist, then his right, letting the loops dangle from his thumbs. The wraps were red and they reminded me of blood running from his wrists.

Should have been a lot of things to say but speaking was proving difficult.

I smelled gunsmoke. Felt the gun in my hand again. But that was just my mind rejecting this reality. The reality of him still existing.

Seconds dragged on.

"I'm glad you came," he said.

That snapped me out of the fog I was in. Glad? How the hell could he be glad?

"I've owed you an apology for a long time."

My fists clenched.

I didn't want to hear this. But he kept on.

68

"Time I served doesn't make up for what I did. I know that. And losing your sister. That's not something I'd have understood then, but I do now. I had a sister once too."

"You don't get to apologize," I said.

He balled up the wraps in his hands and stuffed them one at a time into his shorts pockets. "Understand you feel that way. And I don't ever expect you to want to forgive me, but that doesn't mean I shouldn't ask."

Forgive him. How could he even think that?

"I just came to tell you to stay clear," I said. "You know why it went down the way it did and you know I'll do it again if need be."

"Didn't expect any different. Hoped, maybe, but didn't expect it."

"This some kind of come-to-Jesus experience you had in prison? Is that what you're selling?"

"Done a lot of things I regret. Lost a lot of time. Just trying to use what I have left for better things."

"Why come back here? You request this?"

"Time comes when a man has to face up to what he's done. Can't run because it will always catch up to you."

"I don't want to see you around anywhere."

"Likely you won't."

"I don't want to hear 'likely.' Damned sure better be never."

"You're the one found me."

We stared at each other another long second, then I turned away and headed back the way I came. I paused by the corner though. I looked back. "You said you had a sister. What happened to her?"

"Car wreck. She was only eighteen. Tried to get them parole officials to put me back to then so I could see her one more time, but they wouldn't do it. Said the temptation would be too strong to try to change things. Didn't want me messing with time. I said what's the good of time travel if you can't fix nothing with it? They didn't have much answer for that. Kind of ironic. Only place time travel ever took me was to prison. You know what the guys there like to call it?"

"Time out," I said.

"Yeah. It's time lost though. Because you don't get none of it back."

I took in the sight of him standing there one more time.

Seemed like there ought to be something else to say but there wasn't. So I left.

CHAPTER 15

Cassius. 1984. Eight hours till midnight.

"Who's the girl?" Johnny said.

Cassius glanced up from the rear of the car and noted the blinds shifting at the window of his second-floor apartment. "Nobody."

"That your woman?"

"Nah. Don't worry about her." He put the last shovel in the trunk of the Oldsmobile.

"Sister? Maybe you introduce me later. She fine? She looked good from here."

Cassius slammed the trunk. Johnny "Fastball" McKee was not going to be introduced to his sister. He was going to get in this car and they'd get the hell out of here before the neighbors took notice.

"You drive," Johnny said, and tossed him the keys. Cassius climbed into the driver's seat of the Olds and waited while Johnny finished his cigarette. A school bus went by and a couple of high school girls at the back returned a wave from Johnny. At least the guy didn't smoke in the car. Small victories.

They drove the nine miles without talking. Johnny watched for more high school girls out the window and whistled occasionally, then switched out the tapes in the cassette player. Cassius drove the speed limit, checking the rear view mirror often.

"Why are we doing this in the afternoon? Feels like we ought to wait till dark."

Johnny flicked his lighter open and shut. "I got it handled. Nobody's gonna bother us."

The gate to the Oak Park Cemetery appeared to be locked when they pulled up, and a sign claimed the place was temporarily closed for maintenance. But when Cassius climbed out and checked the chain and combination lock, he found it only half a digit away from coming loose, as promised. He yanked the chain free from the iron bars and pulled the Olds through the gate. It was too damned bright out. At least it was quiet. He relocked the gate and scanned the silent grounds one more time before climbing back into the driver's seat.

"You know where it is from here?" he asked.

Johnny jerked his chin. "Past the hill. I'll tell you when to stop."

"Why we the only ones doing this?"

Johnny sniffed. "Safer this way. You add people, you add problems. That's what Mickey says."

Cassius flexed his hands against the wheel as they drove. The white scars on his knuckles stood out in the sunlight. He drove slow. Already enough disrespect to the dead going to happen. Didn't need to add to it.

The grave was where Johnny said it would be. Under the canopy of an oak with its gown of Spanish moss. At least there'd be shade.

Johnny opened a notebook and checked the dates on the headstone. Then he closed the book. "Get the shovels."

By the time they made it three feet deep, Cassius was dripping with sweat. It was a humid day with no breeze. His shirt clung to his back. He was glad he'd slung his good sweatshirt onto the hood of the car to keep it clean. He was getting filthy down here.

Johnny dug poorly and took frequent breaks. Cassius persisted. This wasn't any tougher than boxing training, and the sooner it was done the better.

They were at five feet when the golf cart appeared. The security guard's belly obscured the front of his belt, but the pistol at his hip was still visible. Had he ever used it out here? Who would he shoot that wasn't already dead?

Johnny climbed out of the hole and met him. Passed the envelope of cash. The security guard watched for a while, then moved on.

"How much does he get?" Cassius asked.

"Don't worry. Your cut is bigger on account of the digging."

Cassius scooped another shovelful into the bucket and Johnny hauled it up by a rope to dump out.

Johnny grunted as he unloaded the dirt onto a pile. "Can't wait till this is done, I'm going to finally take my trip. Did I tell you, they got this bar now. Place you stay at, hotel or whatever? Whole thing goes places. Other times. Past, future, all of it. That's where I'm going. Call it the Rose . . . Rose . . . something. Guess you'd like it."

"Cassius Rose" had always been his fight name. Roses on his gear. Big white one on his lucky hoodie. Looked cool to have a logo. Having style was part of the fight.

Johnny had his wallet out. He pulled a card from it. "See this? That's my invitation. They don't hand out many of those, let me tell you. But I already got my tickets waiting."

Cassius looked up from his digging. "How far's the place go?"

"No joke, I heard you can go see knights and shit. When I get

73

donc with this job tonight, that's what I'm doing. Gonna get me a sword, go back in time, and tear shit up." Johnny swung an imaginary sword with both hands. "When I'm done being a knight, I'm gonna get medieval with some of them old time bar wenches. You know what I'm saying?"

Cassius shook his head and kept digging.

"You don't believe me? Look at this right here." Johnny pulled out the device in his pocket that he called a phone. It didn't look like any phone Cassius had ever seen, but all these guys seemed to have one. Supposedly it didn't work properly in this decade, but it had a camera and all kinds of things on it. Johnny tapped something on the screen and showed him. "That's the place. The Rose 'n Bridge. It's coming tonight. It just shows up where it wants. Picks people up, then it's gone. Poof. Check out this babe that runs the place. Better believe I'm going to get with that." The picture was of some blonde bombshell. Way out of Johnny's league, but Cassius wouldn't be the one to say so.

It was a whole other world. Three weeks ago, if anyone had said he'd be part of a secret society of people who could travel through time, Cassius would have called them mental. But here he was. Picked. Chosen. He had a chance to be part of it all. He wasn't about to mess it up. So he dug.

Thud.

Thud thud.

Johnny leaned over the hole to see.

Cassius worked faster as the top of the casket was exposed. He grabbed a broom and swept some of the dirt away.

It would be tougher from here, making room around the casket, enough to get it open. But they were close. The lid showed the scars of other shovels.

So much for respect.

The sun was down by the time he'd made enough space to pry the top half of the lid up. It was getting harder to see.

Johnny squatted at the edge of the hole and shone a flashlight.

The lid came up with a creak and a moan.

The casket was empty with the exception of the waterproof tarp covering something at the bottom.

Cassius laid on his belly to reach down and pull away the tarp. As he did, Johnny's light illuminated the stacked metal bars beneath.

"Hell yeah," Johnny said. Then he whooped.

Cassius stared at the glint of gold and leaned farther into the darkness toward the foot of the casket. Had to be thirty bars in here.

Hol-lee shit.

Johnny lit a cigarette and smiled. "No matter how many times I see this, it never gets old." He took a drag and let the smoke jet from his nose. "That's gonna be my new motto. *Gold don't get old.* Let's load it up."

CHAPTER 16

Greyson. 1984.

The Rose 'n Bridge tavern crowd was reserved when I walked in the door. Couldn't blame them. Sign up for an exclusive tour of the past, wind up witnesses in a shooting. Not likely to make the marketing brochure.

I'd chosen to arrive the day after the incident but it was all plenty fresh on the guests' minds. Didn't help that the fate of Cassius Roseland was unknown to them. These people didn't know if they'd just watched someone die. When Temporal Crimes eventually publicized that he did die, all their worst suspicions about me would be confirmed.

Heavens wasn't behind the bar. Instead, a newer bartender named Violet was pouring drinks. But when I made my way upstairs and knocked on Heavens' door, she opened it. She leaned on the door jamb.

I had my hands in my pockets. "Still want me for a neighbor?"

She stepped back and held the door open. "You'd better come in."

Her room was better decorated than mine. Wasn't sure how long she'd been a resident at the Rose 'n Bridge but she'd settled in well. Her personal bookshelves rivaled the guest library downstairs. The white rose I'd found in the hallway had made it back upstairs and now sat in a real vase on the kitchen table. The room was cozy and smelled good. Not unlike its owner. Heavens had a wool sweater on and she nestled into the armchair near the bookshelf. Left me a choice of the dormer window seat or a kitchen chair. Window seat had a sleeping cat on it so I took the kitchen chair. I could've used a drink but she hadn't offered. So I sat.

"You were an angry teenager," Heavens said.

"Aren't all teenagers angry?"

"But we don't give them guns to work out their problems."

I scratched at my chin. "I'm sorry you had to be the one on duty that night."

"Last night," she clarified. "Does he die?"

"He actually lived. But Time Crimes is going to publicize that he's dead. Get some people off his scent for a while. Needs to stay a secret."

She was still staring hard at me but she gave the slightest of nods. She knew how things worked. Secrets were secrets for a reason. She'd be good to her word. Her outing Cassius was the least of my worries anyway. But I wanted her to know.

I fidgeted with the chronometer on my wrist. "So, should I pack my bags?"

Heavens crossed her arms and hugged herself. "Official word from the Rosen family is that you are banned from the premises. But it's a younger version of Rosen enforcing a ban on a younger version of you. You know how that works out."

"Where does that leave me? Current age."

Heavens sighed. "*Older* Rosen said you were welcome to stay after the Attu case so you're still welcome. It's complicated, but what isn't around here. I expect you'll get your share of strange looks from patrons, especially on this tour. If you want to skip the rest of this trip, I don't think it would hurt anyone's feelings."

"I can take a few days, check on my offices. Maybe I'll take a case or two for some linears. Let this breathe."

"Are you going to tell me why you shot him?"

"Gets complicated."

She shrugged. "I think I'd rather know."

I shifted on my seat. "I was angry. Wanted revenge. Less than an hour before he showed up at the tavern, he shot my sister, took her chronometer. She died in my arms."

"Thought it might be something like that. I'm sorry, Grey."

"You can tell me it was the wrong response if you want. But I'd do it again."

"I don't know what I'd do in that situation, so I'm hardly one to judge."

"She didn't deserve it. She was the better of the two of us. Whole life ahead of her."

Heavens picked at the sleeve of her sweater. "I've never met her. Would I have liked her?"

"Most do."

We sat like that for nearly a minute, Heavens quiet. Her eyes were moving though. Mind working.

"You have more questions."

She looked back to me. Mouth tense. Something she wasn't saying.

Didn't surprise me that she was drawing deeper conclusions. You didn't get hired for a job like hers unless you could work all the angles. Heavens took a building full of rich tourists all over time. She'd run across any number of paradox-inducing situations and avoided them. Took a mind sharper than most. Now she was staring hard at me.

"You can ask," I said.

"I've met Greyson. The other one."

My duplicate.

"He's tied to this too, isn't he."

But it wasn't a question.

She was thinking it through.

Walking into the tavern and shooting Cassius Roseland had been my revenge. It hadn't changed anything. There was no duplicating of anyone. No changes to the timeline. No reason there would be another version of me walking around as a result.

But there was one. Professor Travers. Living a life with no blood on his hands.

She crossed her arms, hugging herself again.

"I should go." I stood. Walked to the door.

"Piper," she said. The name was almost a whisper. "She's alive still too, isn't she."

But it still wasn't a question.

I opened the door. "Goodbye, Heavens."

CHAPTER 17

Cassius. 1984. 12 hours till midnight.

Cassius Roseland studied himself in the mirror. Could he see any difference? He was as strong as he'd ever been, muscles defined by years in the ring. He pressed his fingertips to his cheeks. He supposed he looked his age. Twenty-seven this month. He pinched the skin at his jaw between two fingers, examining. Would the gravitite treatment make him age any differently? The guys had laughed at some of his other questions so he hadn't asked that.

Time travel.

Somewhere inside him, those crazy blue particles waited, ready to displace him from time.

Whoever would have thought that a guy like him would find himself part of a crew of time travelers?

Hadn't even been that hard.

Bit of a hit to the ego maybe, Mickey asking him to take that dive.

The incentive wasn't hard to see though. Everybody knew

Mickey had money and influence. Anyone who was anybody around here owed it to Mickey somewhere along the line.

He knew fighters who had taken Mickey's money before. It got around, ruined their chances to make it big. But they were doing all right. Mickey took care of his crew. That's what they said.

Cassius had made it look good. Probably too good. That sixth round had been brutal. Might not have even needed to fake it. He was taking some big hits. He probed the scar at his eyebrow. It had taken a stitch to close it. Healed up good enough now though.

He shrugged into his fight night sweatshirt, checked his watch.

At least another hour till Johnny would be there to get him.

He'd grab some lunch out. Why not? He had some money now. More after today.

The shovels were already by the door.

Wasn't sure how he felt about digging up a grave. That's weird shit. But Johnny had promised there was no body in it. Just a payday.

He took one last look at himself in the mirror, then grabbed his keys from the counter.

The phone rang before he reached the door.

He pocketed his keys and walked back across the kitchen, plucking the mustard yellow handset from its cradle.

"Yeah, who is it?"

"Cass, it's me."

His chest tightened.

"What's wrong?"

"I'm okay. I just had to leave school early. Can I stay at your place tonight?"

Cassius sighed. "Why can't you go home?"

"It's *not* home, Cass. That asshole, Kent, is going to light into me again for getting another detention and I can't take it right now. Please can I come to your place?"

"I'm going out."

"I'll use my spare key, sleep on the couch."

"That Family Services lady is going to flip her shit again."

"One night, Cass. Please. He's already been drinking today."

He shifted the handset to his other ear to check his watch again. "I've got a big job today. You come soon or you don't come."

"Bus will be here any minute. I can be there in half an hour. Thanks, big brother."

She hung up.

Cassius put the handset back.

He didn't need another run-in with that uppity social services lawyer again. Sure didn't want to have to beat the shit out of another foster parent for laying hands on his sister either. He flexed his knuckles.

Eighteen months and she would be out of the system. But that was a long time when you were staying with a belligerent closet drunk.

When this was over, he'd have enough cash to get a decent lawyer. Get custody like she wanted. Then they'd be free to make their own way.

Maybe Mickey could see to letting her get that particle treatment too.

Imagine how far they could run then.

Cassius smiled at that thought.

He opened his front door and headed out.

A quarter mile to the Burger King.

There was a McDonald's closer but that smiley girl who gave him free fries didn't work at the McDonald's.

So he'd walk a little farther.

Her name tag said Angela but he wondered if that's what she called herself. Was she waiting for him to ask her out? Probably.

But he'd be closer to the bus stop too. He could maybe see his sister get off the bus there, get her settled before Johnny came to pick him up for the job. He'd have to figure out what she'd done at school without scaring her off. But he was good at that. He could relate. Teachers had never liked him either, but his sister was different. Her smart mouth got her in trouble but only because she *was* so smart. Smarter than half those teachers probably. But like hell if he was going to see her blow it and go down the road he had.

He caught his reflection in a store window. Checked his hair. Looked good. He hoped Angela had a shift today.

A tall, messy-looking white kid across the street was staring at him in the reflection.

Pretty sure he'd never seen him around the neighborhood before. What was his problem?

Cassius walked on.

He looked back once and the kid was still there on the other side of the street. Still watching.

Bunch of weirdos showing up in the neighborhood these days. He was going to move out of here soon as he could.

He cut the corner of the block near the Fotomat. Walking around the back side of the K-Mart he'd come out right in the parking lot for Burger King.

Hands in his hoodie pockets, he'd made it halfway around the back of the store when that tall kid stepped from behind a dumpster.

"What the hell?" Cassius muttered and glanced behind him. This kid have a twin or something? How'd he get here so fast?

The kid's eyes were red. Was he crying? Shit. That was blood all over him.

"Hey, man, you good?" Cassius asked.

The kid pulled a pistol from his dirty coat and raised it. "No. I'm not."

Cassius put his hands up. "Hey man, hey. I ain't got no drugs."

Kid had a two-handed grip on the gun but he was shaking.

"What the hell, man? Be careful with that shit."

"I know you don't know it yet, but you're a killer. You killed my sister today. And it's the last mistake you're going to make."

"The fuck? No I didn't."

"You're going to. So I'm not sorry for this."

"Whoa! Hey."

The blast from the gun was loud.

Cassius staggered from the impact.

Holy shit. Crazy junkie kid just shot him. He looked down at the hole in his sweatshirt. Oh God. That wasn't a good place to get shot.

He felt weak. Went down to one knee. Shit.

He looked up and the kid was still there, staring at him. He'd lowered the smoking gun. His lip was quivering. Tears coming out both eyes. The kid wiped one away with the back of his hand. "I'm not sorry. She deserves to live. Now she will."

Cassius felt the warm wetness spreading on his chest. What had he said? Later today he was supposed to kill somebody? Why?

The kid put the gun back in his coat and pushed his sleeve up. He had a fancy watch. He did something to it. Turned something. But then he waited, watching.

Cassius fell over, rolling onto his back.

Smelled like cardboard back here. He could smell the Burger King too. He wondered if Angela would ever hear about this. Would she wonder what happened to him?

He wished he could tell her. Tell anybody.

He should have known it was all too good to be true. Fucking time travel.

Somewhere far off he heard a city bus.

There was something he wanted to say but he couldn't get anything out.

His eyelids fluttered. He looked for the crying kid with the gun again, but he was gone.

And damn. Now he was too.

PART 2
NADIA

CHAPTER 18

Greyson. 2019. Timeline 1.

The emails in my inbox were all whiny. Guy wanted his girlfriend followed. Insurance company wanted video of a supposedly disabled guy playing sports. Old lady wanted me to find out who was letting a dog poop on her lawn every night.

There were a number of social media search requests also. Online background checks. I set Waldo on those and he'd email some results to clients without me having to worry about it. Easy money, but not much of it.

I swiveled in my chair and took in the view of Central Avenue out the window for a bit. I swiveled back.

It was only half past eleven and the bottle of Bulleit in the bottom desk drawer was already sounding like a good idea. I walked downstairs instead and visited the burrito place next door. Hard to have a burrito without a beer though. So I had one. Lime for authenticity. Second beer was just to keep the first one company.

St. Pete felt hot today. What was it, summer? I checked my phone calendar. Late spring. Close enough.

Maybe I'd take in the sights.

I drove the Boss with the windows down, visited the local soccer fields on the previous Thursday night and shot some video. Found a woman and followed her to a piano lesson and a yoga class and to serving lunch at the Ronald McDonald House for the families of sick kids. Watched her work hard at her job and go to a well-deserved girls night, and finally walked up to her while she was having a martini at The Canopy.

I handed her a printed copy of an email. "Idiot guy you're dating thinks you're cheating on him because you're so busy. Hired me to follow you. And, oh yeah." I held up my phone. "Here's a photo of his other girlfriend he hasn't told *you* about."

She wasn't upset. Had a feeling he was a waste of her time. Her friends all agreed and looked relieved. They'd wanted to tell her. They invited me to stay for a drink. So I had one. Took one for the road too.

I walked ten blocks into the neighborhood where I lived and planted a few cameras around an old lady's yard on the way. I had a buzz on from the drinks so the angles were sloppy but I wasn't trying to be Ansel Adams.

Just as I got home to my apartment, I had a ping from the cameras. I checked the feed. Sure enough, guy was leaving his dog's deposit on the lawn. No bag in sight. This was going to be a quick resolution. But a black cat came racing up to me as I put away my phone. It got priority.

"What's up, Hawk? You miss me?" I took a knee to pet him.

The cat looked only slightly more battle-worn than last I'd seen him. A couple new scratches around his ears. Neighborhood wasn't going to rule itself. I let him rub against my hand and purr for a few minutes before locating a bag of treats in the garage. He became happily absorbed in them so I grabbed what else I needed and walked south again.

When I got to the old lady's yard, I collected my cameras and used a nearby speed limit sign as an anchor to jump back in time twenty-five-and-a-half minutes.

Guy's dog was still mid-squat. The thick mid-thirties white dude was scrolling on his phone.

I took one of the poop bags I'd pulled from my garage and used it on the steaming pile when the guy walked away. He was only a few houses along when I caught up to him. I twisted the timer function on my chronometer and let it start counting down.

"Hey, Sweatpants."

He turned. Surprised to see anyone.

"Forget something?"

I let the poop bag dangle from my hand.

"How about you mind your own business, dickwad."

"That's colorful," I said. "Should have gone with an apology."

He gave me his best scowl. But his dog's tail was wagging. Wanted to sniff me. Didn't blame it. I smelled great.

"T-shirt or pants?" I asked.

"What?"

"I'm giving you options."

I was within reach now. He swelled his chest and stepped closer, getting in my face. "Man, I don't know what kind of nonsense you're talking but I don't need anyone telling me how to—"

"Stay real still, okay?"

"What?"

I reached for his shirt collar with my free hand.

"The hell? Don't touch me." He shoved me. I didn't go far so he balled a fist and swung. Too slow though. I lowered my head and planted a back foot and let him connect with the top of my forehead. His knuckles didn't like that. And he punched like a fifth-grader.

While he was recoiling in pain, I stepped forward and pulled the waistband of his sweats back, dropping the bulk of the poop bag inside his skivvies but hanging on to the very end of the bag.

He grabbed at my arm and tried to back away but I had ahold of his shoulder with my other hand. The dog barked.

I checked my chronometer and addressed the dog. "Don't worry. I was never here."

The countdown on the chronometer finished and I blinked away.

I was standing on the sidewalk alone now. The low-density gravitite treatment of the bag had been enough to bring it along with me, but not the ungravitized contents. Oops.

I straightened and rubbed my forehead. Stretched my neck to one side and checked my chronometer again.

Did I feel better? Maybe.

I looked around, checked my email on my phone. Nothing new. Cases closed?

The leave-the-poop-in-the-asshole's-pants trick used to cheer me up more. But I guess I wasn't twenty-five anymore.

I sighed.

Wondered what Heavens was thinking at the moment. Probably nothing to do with dog poop. Probably more to do with what an angry violent kid I used to be.

I found a dumpster and tossed the empty poop bag in.

Maybe I still was.

And still a killer. Couldn't forget that part. And now she knew.

I walked home.

CHAPTER 19

Nadia. 1984. Timeline 2.

Nadia Roseland stepped off the bus and exhaled. No one had hassled her on the ride and it was a short walk from here to Cass's place.

He didn't have cable but it was still better than the group home. She'd be in a ton of trouble for ditching her last two classes of the day but whatever. Profesora Sanders could make the rest of la clase do sentence diagrams. Hasta la vista, suckers.

The barber shop was busy today. A few men inside looked her way. She slouched a little going by. Why did guys just stare all the time? Not her fault she'd grown another inch and two bra sizes this year. She wasn't even showing any skin.

Old dudes were gross.

A couple twenty-something girls went by in a T-top Firebird. Great perms. Gold hoop earrings. Fuzzy dice on the mirror. Bet they didn't have AP physics homework either.

Two more years.

Not even.

She'd be free. She'd graduate, get a scholarship to city college.

Do well, maybe transfer to the university. And she wouldn't have to listen to that douchebag Kent anymore. How they ever put him in charge of a foster home, she'd never know. Probably banging that child services lady.

Her chess team teacher seemed to think she might even land a scholarship to the university *this* year, even somewhere out of state. But she wasn't holding her breath. Wouldn't be surprised if they'd all found a way to lose her applications.

Still, anywhere was better than the group home.

Cass would help her out. Maybe she'd move in with him for a while. Some of the dudes he worked with looked like creepers, but nobody would bother her as long as Cass was around. He won all his fights. Well, except for that last one. He'd come back though.

Nadia threw a jab and a cross in the air. She'd learned a few moves too. Duck, step, right hook. Not that Cass would ever let her in a ring for real.

"You're the brains of this family. Got to work smarter."

She smiled. He always made her feel like she could do anything. The ten years between them made him seem like a dad some days more than a brother. But she'd be an adult soon too.

She adjusted her grip on her backpack strap. Soon enough.

Wow.

That was a lot of cops.

Must have been eight squad cars parked around the K-Mart with lights on. Ambulances too. Wonder what that was all about.

They didn't have police tape up or anything but it looked like they were keeping people away from the back lot.

A crowd was growing on the sidewalk. People craning their necks. Nadia checked traffic and crossed the street.

Voices were subdued. She had to get close to hear.

One guy was holding his hand over his mouth while he watched.

That one lady was wiping away tears.

Someone hurt bad?

Nadia edged her way through the crowd. Would be a weird place for a car accident. She'd seen a bicyclist get knocked over by the bus one time but didn't know if she wanted to see worse than that. She got to the front. Cops were taking pictures. They moved aside and she had a view of the person on the ground.

All she could see from this angle was the shoes and jeans. Converse basketball shoes like Cass had. His were white too.

He had a sleeveless sweatshirt like that also. But his didn't have red on it.

She stared.

That guy wasn't moving. Like at all.

"So sad," someone near her said.

"I've seen him around," another replied. "At the corner store. And jogging."

"I think he was a boxer."

"That's right. I saw him on a poster recently. That big fight they hyped up."

Their voices were drowned out by the pounding of her pulse in her ears.

Nadia focused on the area beyond the man's sweatshirt. She couldn't see his face. She took two steps to the side. Then another, pushing past a big lady that had been crying. The cops were moving around. Still couldn't see.

Then she could.

He was staring up at the sky.

Cass.

She froze. Couldn't be. Cass was home.

Cass was home.

She backed up two steps, then four. She turned around and pushed straight through a couple holding hands.

She sprinted along the sidewalk, backpack bouncing on her shoulder. She threw it to the ground.

She ran.

All the way down the street.

Across the grass and up the stairs. Along the porch. She pounded on the door, dug in her pocket. By the time she had the key out her hands were shaking so badly she couldn't fit it in the keyhole.

Cass was inside. Cass was inside.

She got the key in the door and fought it. Deadbolt too. The doorknob slammed into the wall when she shoved the door open.

"Cass?"

Kitchen. Dining room. Then bedroom, bathroom.

Please no.

Please be here.

The front door was still open. She rushed back onto the porch. Hands in her hair. Looked down the hall toward the coin laundry.

Her whole body shook.

He'd just stepped out for a minute. He'd be back. That couldn't have been him. She took a few steps away from the railing. Went inside. She didn't get the door closed all the way. Didn't make it to a chair. She collapsed on the kitchen floor, her back to the fridge. That ugly mustard phone hung on the wall. She'd called him on that phone half an hour ago and he'd answered.

Cass had been home.

She was still staring at the phone when the knock jolted her. The cops already?

But the man that stepped into the room didn't look like a cop. Cops didn't wear track suits.

"Yo, Cassius. You in here or what?" He looked at the shovels stacked near the door. Rested a hand on one.

The man had a pistol in his waistband. Gold chain around his neck.

Finally the man's eyes fell on her. He stared, then his mouth formed a smile. "Well, hello there, gorgeous."

She'd seen him before. Someone Cass worked with?

He kept his distance but crouched to be on her level. "Hey, you got something to say, beautiful? Where's Cassius? Him and me got some work to do today."

She hadn't let herself cry. Because it would mean she admitted it was true. But with this man staring at her she couldn't pretend. He'd invaded her reality. And there was no way to hold back the flood. Her body betrayed her, trembling. The tears came and she wailed. Nothing was real anymore.

The world had collapsed. Sky falling in on her.

She shuddered. Spasmed.

That guy was closer now, Hands out, pulling her to him.

"Hey now, don't cry."

She didn't resist. It didn't matter when the world was broken.

"Cass, Cass . . ."

The stranger held her while she opened her mouth wide and screamed into his shoulder.

"Hey, don't you worry. Johnny's got you. Everything's going to be all right. You're going to be just fine."

As she sobbed, head pressed to his chest, she slowly focused through the tears. She'd soaked his jacket, but he didn't seem to mind. And she didn't care about that now.

All she could see was that shining gun at his waist. One of her tears had landed on the handle. It shimmered there.

For the first time she could remember, she wanted to touch a gun. She wanted to reach out and take it from him. To use it.

Because someone had wrecked her universe.

And she wanted them to die.

CHAPTER 20

Greyson. 2035 Timeline 1.

Jonathan Black Elk was sitting in a wooden rocking chair on the front porch when I got out of the car. If he had his gun I couldn't spot it.

Plenty of years gone by since last I'd seen him. They showed on his face in thick lines etched deep. His hair was still black with some silver at the temples. Had maybe thirty pounds he didn't before but he wore his shirt neatly pressed and tucked into blue jeans. Still struck an imposing figure sitting there.

Maybe it was the old memories mixing with the new. He'd seemed bigger than life then. An old-school lawman.

"Figured you'd come eventually," he said.

I crossed the dirt drive and up the gravel path that led to the porch. Porch had no railing. Nothing to obstruct the view for fifty miles of red desert and rocks.

"Saw the river. Thought maybe you'd be fishing."

He sized me up. "Been down and back already. Had trout for lunch." His eyes drifted to the drive, studying the Boss. Then his gaze came back to me. Waited.

"You lied about where you put Roseland."

"Does it matter? You were going to find him no matter where I put him."

"He knew that?"

Black Elk nodded. "He still alive?"

"So far."

"That's something then." Black Elk gestured to the bottle sitting on the table beside him. "Want a drink?"

I stepped up onto the porch.

"Go in, get yourself a glass. Cupboard above the sink."

I opened the screen door of the cabin and entered, noting the rustic decor. Furniture was well made from local trees. Navajo art on the walls. His gun belt hung from a peg by the door. Pistol wasn't in it.

I retrieved a glass and walked back onto the porch, crossing to the seat on the far side of him.

Black Elk tipped more whiskey into his own glass, then handed me the bottle.

I added a couple fingers worth to mine, then sat. We took in the landscape.

"This your retirement scene?"

"Will be soon. Supposed to be where no one can bother me. You can see how that's working out."

I sipped the whiskey. Smooth.

"I won't stay long."

We stared at the landscape a while longer.

"Whatever's on your mind got you out here won't speak itself. Better out with it."

I swirled the whiskey in my glass. "I need to know when it's over. I'm too close. Can't see it."

"Suppose that depends on you. You saw him. Does it seem over?"

I mulled that. Took another sip. "I'm not just talking about the tavern. That wasn't all that went down that day. I suspect you know that. And I've been living the last fourteen years waiting for an ax to fall that never came. If it's ever going to, I guess I'm ready to get it over with."

"If you came here to give some kind of confession, you're in the wrong place. TCID headquarters is a hundred years from here."

"I just want to know what to expect going forward."

Black Elk sipped his drink and sucked his teeth as it went down. Went back to staring. "Been at this a long time, kid. But I still remember you sitting across the table from me after that tavern shooting. Wired teenager fresh from putting someone down with a .38. Remember the way your eyes looked. All wild and red. We mostly sat you there just to give you a bit of quiet. Quell the rage some."

"You knew why by then?"

"Sure. We'd looked into it before I went in the room with you. Gathered video of Roseland shooting your sister. A few days later we had his full confession in a plea deal."

"You let me walk."

Black Elk nodded. "Remember what I said?"

"You said 'Don't do anything stupid.'"

"Musta used that line five hundred times in my career. Not that anyone listened."

A hawk soared overhead in the breeze, dove for something in the distance and flew off with its prize in its talons.

"Nobody checked up on me," I said.

Black Elk drank some more. "You had a damned chronometer stashed somewhere you could use to jump through time. We knew the moment you walked out you'd be in the wind. Wasn't a point in trying to track you down."

"You had to know where I'd go."

"Had some educated guesses."

"So why not come after me?"

"You hadn't done anything illegal."

"You didn't think I was a public threat?"

"Public? No. You were a threat to Cassius Roseland, but that was it."

"But you still let me go."

"We held you till sunup. Wherever you went that morning, however you got yourself there, and whatever you did after wasn't TCID business. Nobody asked us to follow you. Nobody called and told us to investigate anything after. So we didn't."

"Just that simple."

"You did some law enforcement training, I hear?"

"Did a linear academy. Never joined up after. I didn't fit the mold."

"But you met enough cops. Did the work, set up your own shop. You know at least some of what our job is. People seem to think that because we're Time Crimes we have all the answers. Think time travel solves everything. But you know that's a joke. Because when you have to police an entire multiverse, you have a multiverse of problems that come with it.

"One week I was working three separate cases of child trafficking with kids getting stolen from the past and sold upstream to rich folks in a timeline where everyone started going sterile. Same week we had drug dealers from the future showing up killing people they thought would be eventual competition. Also we had this case where a guy kept jumping in and out of old linear women's bedrooms buck naked and giving them heart attacks. Turns out there were six different versions of this guy we ended up with. Every one a pervert. That was just one week in this job. Now think about how much time we thought we should invest keeping an eye on you so you wouldn't do something violent to a guy we knew worked for the local mob and already had up on murder charges."

"He was expendable."

"He was the least of our worries at the time. And truth be told, none of the folks at TCID lose sleep if another gravitized goon for the other side stops showing up for work. One less gun we have to watch for next time we show up on a bust."

I polished off the rest of the whiskey in my glass. Black Elk offered the bottle again but I waved it away.

He added to his glass, then set the bottle down. "I ran into some of your family one time. Mom, dad, some event somewhere. Can't remember which. But your sister was there. One I knew had been killed. The brother too. You, but not you. I looked you in the eyes and knew you'd never seen me in your life. So I knew there was a timeline somewhere where those two never ran into Cassius Roseland. Now, did it bother me to see a couple young people living their life like normal folk, never touched by that kind of bloodshed? You think I felt that pretty young girl ought to be dead?"

"No. You didn't."

Black Elk nodded. "You are correct." He sipped his drink some more.

"So that's it. Nobody's coming."

"You been living your life waiting for it. That's some punishment in itself. That why you drive around solo, getting yourself beat up solving other people's messes? Penance?"

"There was nothing else for me. Nothing that helped me sleep at night. Figured it would have come to an end by now, but it hasn't."

"Guilt?"

"No. I'd do it again. Piper deserved to live. But I might do it differently."

"If it's weighing on your conscience, I imagine an officer somewhere would listen to you. But don't expect a thank you. More than a few agents I know at TCID figure you're doing the

Lord's work out here. Heard about enough of your cases. Might be unconventional methods, but you're taking bad guys off the street and taking your lumps to do it. You may not be on exactly the same team but you're at least on the same side. Be sure you're sure before you decide to bench yourself."

I set my glass on the table between our chairs and stood. Black Elk did too.

"Thanks for the drink."

"Apparently you know where to find me. Come by when you get some peace on this and we'll have another one."

I nodded and headed toward the car. I made it about halfway.

"Hey, Travers," Black Elk called from the porch.

I turned.

"Don't do anything stupid."

CHAPTER 21

Mickey Twitch. 1984. Timeline 2.

Mickey Twitch checked his watch. This whole situation was eating into his afternoon.

Across the desk in his office stood Johnny Fastball and this girl he'd dragged in. Would have been a looker without the puffy eyes from crying. But not at the moment. Of course Johnny would bring her in. You could always count on Johnny to go scooping up the young ones. Guy needed to grow up. But the brother being dead was bothersome.

Now the operation was behind schedule, and Mickey didn't like that. New York wouldn't like it either.

"We're gonna find out what happened to your brother, all right?" He tried to sound sympathetic. Didn't come out too good.

"When?"

She had focus, this kid. He could give her that. Wasn't crying now. Looked like she wanted to knife somebody.

"Mickey always takes care of his people," Johnny said, his arm still around her. "Cassius was one of us, so you're going to be too. Ain't that right, Mick."

Mickey gave the girl his most reassuring smile. It faded when he looked at Johnny.

Johnny was getting too casual calling him Mick. The stones on this guy. Showing off for the girl.

Cassius Roseland had been a losing bet, apparently. Mickey had scored when the guy'd taken that dive, but bringing him into the operation might have been a stretch. Johnny liked the guy, figured he was good for digging on this job. Certainly had the muscles. But a lot of good that did them now. Guy was dead.

And now this chick had turned up. Suppose he ought to be grateful it wasn't a whole blubbering family.

Mickey's stomach growled again. This was his lunchtime. He wished he'd left before these two walked in.

"You're gonna take her someplace, then you're gonna get back to work. Gino will fill in."

"Sure thing. Oh. Cassius had the shovels."

Mickey rested his elbows on the desk. "You telling me we don't have *shovels*?"

Johnny rubbed his neck. "Had Cassius pick some up but they're still at his place. You had me pitch ours. After the last time."

That was true. He had said that.

"So you go back to the fighter's place, you get the shovels. Or you go to the store. What the fuck ever. But get the job done fast."

He looked at the girl. "Excuse my French."

She just stared at him.

Johnny nodded. "No problem, Mick. I'll take her back to my place quick. I'll get Gino. We'll get it done."

"When do you find out who killed my brother?" the girl asked.

There was that focus again. She looked smart, this kid. Maybe she'd have some uses.

He would have to find out about the dead guy getting

105

popped. Maybe it had nothing to do with him. Maybe the fighter was in with some shit he didn't know about. He'd have to check. But after lunch.

"We'll let you know soon. We have our ways."

"I want to be involved," she said. "I want to know who it was."

"So you will be. Then what? You want I give you a gun and you blow the guy's head off? I don't think that's what you want."

"What if I do?"

"I think you watch too many movies."

Kids these days.

But she was intense. He'd give her that.

He waved Johnny away.

Girl went with him.

This was a big day. Big operation. Forty-six million in gold bars from that London airport job in circulation. Relocate it safely for New York and they'd trust him with the bigger jobs. Big time future money kinda jobs.

His operation was small but he liked it that way. Fewer people knew what was what the better. You add people, you add problems.

Like now he had a dead guy. Could be nothing. Could be a problem. He'd figure it out after lunch.

When Johnny and the girl were well gone, he locked the office door and peeked through the blinds. The warehouse was quiet. He took the painting of the stupid boat off the wall and stared at the wall safe.

Now what the hell was that combo?

The keypad on the safe glowed. He used to think it was cool. A safe from the future had seemed like a good idea since nobody in 1984 was going to crack it. But stupid thing made him change the password every thirty days. His finger hovered over the pad. How was he supposed to remember it, changing so often? He started to press a button and swore. He went to his desk, pulled out the center drawer and felt around above it till he found the piece of paper wedged up there. He glanced at the door, then unfolded the paper. Last password was scribbled there below a half dozen crossed out ones. Oh yeah. Now he remembered. He folded the paper up and shoved it back.

When he got the safe open, the Temprovibe was there, waiting for him. So was the anchor. It was just a sawed-off chunk of hand rail but it was his favorite these days.

He fitted the Temprovibe to his arm, plugged in the destination on his keypad. A timeline only he ever went. Some peace and fucking quiet.

The Temprovibe gave him an error message. Previously used. The hell? He tried again. Same result. He swore at it and looked for more available times. Twenty minutes later. Fine. Restaurant would be busier. He didn't like that, but whatever. He was getting hungry. He selected the time he was offered and activated the device. His skin got all tingly like it always did as he touched the anchor. The Temprovibe started its countdown.

Shit. He'd almost forgot his piece. He reached over and pulled the pistol from the drawer, pocketing it in his jacket. There we go. All ready.

He went.

Walking out of the men's room in the back of the restaurant, he ran his hand over his hair. If that new waitress gave him the eye again today he'd get her number. Take her someplace fancy.

Bet she'd never done it with a time traveler before.

He straightened his jacket as he made his way past some tables, working his way toward his favorite booth. She woulda saved it for him. She knew he'd be here today.

But as he approached the booth he frowned. Waitress had her back to him.

Some jabroni was in his seat.

This was unacceptable. Place was filled up. What was he supposed to do, wait for another table up front like a schmuck?

He kept walking toward his spot.

Hang on. She was writing something on her little pad. Was that her phone number?

She tore it off, handed it over.

This son of a bitch. Guy wanted to take his spot on his special day? Ask out his girl? Had another thing coming.

When the waitress turned around her smile faded and her eyes widened. Looked goofy with her mouth open.

"Don't bother takin' this guy's order," Mickey said. "He's leaving."

But then she stepped aside and he had a good look at the guy.

Aww shit.

Somebody had messed up.

Guy in the booth was him.

CHAPTER 22

Mickey Twitch. 1984. His private timeline.

Mickey Twitch sat across the table from his other self and listened to the damned waitress go on about the situation. She didn't know he had a twin. Wow they even dressed alike. She knew some twins but none as identical as them.

He smiled politely till she left with his drink order, then he leveled his gaze at his doppelgänger.

"Seems we got ourselves a situation."

His other self had to be none-too-pleased about the circumstances either, but he'd finished a drink or two and had the waitress's number, so maybe that could account for him looking nonplussed.

Mickey was boiling.

"Nobody knows this spot but me. This timeline is clean. So we both end up here like this, it's no good. Somebody fucked up."

"Had to be you," his other self said. He slurped his drink.

"Says who? You're here same as me."

"You do something unusual today?"

"Same routine. Same shit different day." Mickey leaned

forward and lowered his voice. "You got the big job going down for New York?"

"Couple guys on it. Keeping it low key. Should be wrapped up by sundown."

Same then.

Mickey had heard of situations like this with time travel. Key was to get things straight quick, figure out the glitch and prevent the oddities from spreading. If things got too weird it would bring the time cops investigating. Right now they were safe enough, in an isolated timeline, just a couple twin brothers not bothering nobody. But back where they came from was a different matter. Something was wrong there and they had to figure it out quick before the whole timestream fractured or some shit.

Better run through it.

"Was up usual time, coffee, paper, cigarette on the veranda. Candace was yappin' at me. Naggin' about that tree needs trimming in the yard. That you too?"

His other self nodded.

"Did the crossword. Didn't finish it."

"Forty-seven across," his duplicate said. "Academic purist? What kind of clue is that?"

"Only six letters. We shoulda been able to figure that out. But that's not my point. It happened to you too."

His other self conceded it. "I went to work. Banged Claudia."

"She's a terrible receptionist. Misses half the calls."

"Maybe 'cause we got her in the office shaggin' so much."

Mickey shrugged. "Maybe." The waitress came back with his drink and handed his other self his plate of meatball lasagna. She then looked expectantly at him.

"What you think?" He pointed to the meatball lasagna.

"Really?" she asked.

What. She was looking down at him now for being

unoriginal? He couldn't take this nonsense. "You know what? Fine. Gimme the goddamn chicken penne one."

"With pesto?" she asked.

"Of course with the pesto. You think I'm some kind of guy don't eat pesto?"

She made her note, then walked off. She wasn't giving him the sexy eyes anymore.

"Maybe be nicer, huh?" his other self said. "Still trying to hit that over here."

"You want to focus maybe? We got bigger problems right now."

Other Him shrugged and dug into his meatball lasagna. Looked damned good. Mickey shoulda asked for a second plate. But not like the other him had offered to share. What a dick this guy was.

"So we had a regular morning. Till Johnny showed up with that girl."

His other self looked up, cheese hanging from his lip. He spoke with his mouth full. "What girl?"

"Girl whose brother got shot. The fighter."

Other Him screwed up his face. "Cassius? Thought you said he was on the job?"

"Yeah, originally. Not after getting dead obviously. Gino and Johnny are on it now."

Other Him chewed a while.

"That didn't happen to you?" Mickey pressed.

"No. Johnny called and told me he was picking up Cassius for the job right before I came here. No problems."

"That's our glitch then," Mickey said. "In my time somebody iced the fighter. Yours they didn't."

"Why'd they do him in yours?"

"The hell should I know."

"It's your day."

"You think I had my own guy whacked on a day I need him? Think that's how I get business done? I'm you, shithead."

Other Him bit into another meatball. "My guy didn't get iced."

Smug bastard.

Mickey frowned. They had to figure this out.

Things going normal in his other self's day didn't make him feel any better about the situation. Something was going sideways. New York not getting their shipment on time would ruin his reputation. They'd counted on him to get the job done with no fuss.

Now this other self had a leg up on that.

But hang on. Did this other him not see the opportunity this might present? Two of them meant this paradox was making duplicates. Two of him, but what else? Two Johnnys, two of this Cassius mope. Two different digs for the gold?

If New York got their millions on schedule from this other him, how would they know to miss the pile Johnny and Gino would be digging up? They were in a different timeline now. Maybe this fighter getting snuffed out wasn't such a bad thing for him.

'Course New York might figure it out. Then he'd be in some shit.

Could be a stupid idea. Maybe he ought to play it straight.

But that was a lot of fucking gold.

Waitress finally showed up with his chicken penne. He dug in. Not bad. It was no meatball lasagna though. Been looking forward to that all morning. At least she'd brought him another drink.

Other Him kept flirting with her. Putting a hand on her leg. This shit somehow worked for him? Bet this wasn't how he'd look doing it. He'd play it cooler, let her chase him. See? There she went, while Other Him sat there with a stupid expression on his face and a boner under the table.

They ate in silence for a bit.

When the girl brought the check for the meal, they both stared at each other.

"You know what? I got this," his other self said, reaching for the book thingy she'd put it in.

Showing off for her. The generous brother. Fine. Whatever. You stuff all that lasagna in your face and not share a bite you deserve to pay, you selfish prick.

They got up from the table together. Other Him had unbuttoned the top of his pants. Blew the waitress a kiss on the way out.

Seriously?

Mickey led the way back to the bathroom and opened the door. His other self hung back.

"What?" Mickey asked. "You worried about walking in a bathroom with another guy and your new girlfriend thinking you're a homo or something?"

"What? No."

"You really gotta work on your sense of self, you know that?"

"This what I get for buying lunch? How about a thank you?"

"After you, your fucking generous highness," Mickey said, and held the door open.

His other self walked through.

Mickey stepped inside too and locked the door behind him. His other self was already taking his jacket off, exposing the Temprovibe on his arm.

"This part we got to be careful about, right? I don't want to accidentally jump back to the timeline where you left things all screwed up." Other Him reached into his jacket and rummaged around. "I think I brought that analyzer. One can tell our different time signatures apart. That'll keep us straight going back."

Mickey reached into his jacket too. But he didn't pull out the temporal frequency analyzer. He pulled out his piece. He aimed the pistol at the back of his other self's head and squeezed the trigger.

Other Him knocked over the trash can when he fell. Spilled a bunch of paper towels out. They started turning red while he laid there.

Mickey put away his gun.

Pedant. That's what it was. Six letters. Academic purist. Why hadn't he been able to come up with that before? He'd fill it in when he got home.

He collected the Temprovibe from the arm of his other self and took the temporal ground analyzer from the guy's hand too. The thing *would* be useful. He used it on the body and recorded the timestream signature. He'd need that. Had a lot of jumping back and forth to do now.

Gonna have to sort this mess out.

He checked his other self's wallet and extracted the ID and cash. The number from the waitress was in there too, scribbled on her little notepad paper. He considered it for a second, then balled it up and tossed it into the urinal on the wall.

Never coming back here now.

He'd find this place again in another timeline when the job was done.

And he'd order himself the goddamn meatball lasagna.

CHAPTER 23

Greyson. 2019. Timeline 1.

My knuckles were starting to swell, even under the wraps. Should have used the bag gloves.

I took a step back from the heavy bag hanging from my garage ceiling and dripped sweat on the floor. I'd managed a five mile run and thirty minutes rotating between the speed bag, heavy bag, and pushups.

The chin-up bar was supposed to be next but I was spent. I unwrapped my hands.

Shower time.

I made for the exterior stairs that went up the side of my garage apartment, but Hawk was sitting there staring at me from the sixth step, scorn in his eyes.

I stared back.

"Ugh. Okay fine," I said.

I turned around and went back into the garage. I jumped for the chin-up bar and did a full hang before forcing myself up. Two. Five. Big exhale. Keep going. Eight. Nine. Come on, you son of a bitch. Ten.

My shoulders burned.

So I stood there for thirty seconds and then did it again.

This time up the stairs Hawk gave me a look of temporary tolerance.

"Never going to be as tough as you, buddy. I've come to terms with it."

When I got to the door, he followed, stopping at the top stair and meowing.

I retrieved the tin of cat treats from the basket I kept inside the door and portioned some out onto the cement stair railing. He hopped up and made short work of them. Payment for coaching services rendered.

I took too long in the shower, just letting the water run over me. I cooled it down by increments till it was running cold over my sore muscles. I had a fresh oversized towel waiting. After I dried off, I slid into a t-shirt and jeans straight from the dryer.

Didn't know how to get any cleaner.

It was a decent start.

The apartment was clean too. I'd arisen in the morning and done the surfaces and floors. Trash and recycling out. Fresh bags in everything. Sheets changed. Place smelled like a potpourri forest.

But I still had a mess to clean up. This was surface level.

I was delaying the inevitable.

I oiled my gun next. Laying out the parts on towels on the dining room table, reassembling everything and checking the load. Double-checked the redundant safety measures with both my chip ring and palm print. It unlocked instantly each time. Ready for action.

What now?

Lunch wouldn't hurt.

I let the bottom slice of bread sizzle in the skillet while I portioned out the protein in slices. Pickle, mustard, nut-based cheese. I had the thing assembled on the skillet and had just flipped it when Waldo chimed from the speaker on the wall.

"What is it, homie?"

"An alert has been sent from your office in 1995. Someone is looking to speak with you."

"Eager repeat client?"

"No. It's Manuel Del Toro."

"Manuel?" I looked down at the skillet. "Guy who makes these sandwiches better than me, Manuel?"

"The kitchen manager from the Rose 'n Bridge. Yes."

"Manuel, who still doesn't like me, Manuel?"

"It would seem he has overcome his aversion to you long enough to locate one of your offices."

"Did he bring his dog?"

"No."

Damn. I liked that dog.

"He say what he wanted?"

"Would you like me to set up a video conference to resolve the rest of your queries?"

"Don't really want him seeing me copying his sandwich."

"I doubt yours will be considered competition."

"How would you know? You don't even have taste buds."

"A fact that has served me well while employed by you."

"Hey, this thing looks delicious if you ask me." I turned off the burner and tipped the sandwich onto a plate.

"So . . . an audio call, perhaps?"

"He's going to be able to tell I'm chewing. He won't like it." I set the skillet in the sink to cool. "We'll go see him after I eat. We can take the Boss."

"You'd like to drive a priceless vehicle through several wormholes in the fabric of space and time, traveling twenty-nine years into the past at considerable energy expense, all to avoid a conversation in which a person who already doesn't like you might hear you chewing?"

"If you were in the sandwich eating business, you'd understand." I took a bite of mine. Chewed. Okay, maybe a tad overdone. Little too mustardy. But it wasn't going to go to waste.

"You were correct on one point," Waldo said. "You do chew loudly."

My office in St. Pete in the 1990s wasn't as nice as the one I had in 2019, but arguably more historic. It was a rented hotel room in The Detroit, an old hotel that had sat in one form of renovation or another on the same spot since 1888. After 1993 they'd stop using the place as a hotel in order to sell condos instead, but for the late eighties and early nineties, it put me in the heart of downtown.

Parking was easier to find then so I had no trouble putting the Boss out front. I located Manuel in the bar downstairs, a grim expression on his face and a beer in his hand.

There were a lot of shoulder pads and old people in here. He didn't really fit in.

He saw me approach and got off his bar stool.

"Not a man I expected to see," I said. "Heard you rang my bell."

"Assumed I'd find you if I waited in the bar long enough."

"I'll take that as a compliment," I said. "Based on my fun-loving personality."

"I didn't come here for fun," Manuel said. "Heavens is missing."

I blinked. "Come again?"

"We can't find her."

"At all? She's the manager of the inn. How do you lose the manager?"

"She went on the excursion. With the tourists. Didn't come back. Nobody knows where she went. Starting to get worried."

"I assume you called her. Checked her room for notes?"

"We called. Left messages. She would have called back by now. We're supposed to be departing with the inn back to next century to pick up another load of tourists, but she missed check-in."

That was bothersome. Time travelers aren't usually late for things. Unless they want to be. Or someone else wants them to be.

"You call Time Crimes?"

"She left me instructions. She said if anything ever happened, and we can't find her, I'm supposed to tell you first."

"When did she say this?"

"After you solved that case with the androids."

"Shit. You think she knew she'd go missing?"

He shrugged. "She said find you. I found you." He set his empty beer bottle on the bar. "What are you going to do about it?"

"Well, find her, obviously." We walked together toward the lobby doors. "She give you any other clues?"

"I'm not the clue guy. That's you."

"Where's the Rose 'n Bridge parked right now?"

He told me.

"Wait there for me. I'll need to come check things out. Keep all the guests there, especially any who were on the 1984 excursion and might have seen her last."

He nodded. Then he sniffed and studied me, eyes narrowing. "You trying to make the sandwich?"

"Maybe?"

He took one more sniff and his nose wrinkled. "Too much mustard. And you overcooked it."

CHAPTER 24

Mickey Twitch. 1984. Timeline 2.

Mickey watched the New York guys count the gold bars for the third time, then glanced toward the duffel bag of cash he'd be getting in return. Looked light.

Utter bullshit when you thought about it.

No wonder so many people in this business got shot.

But he kept his face impassive.

The beady-eyed guy in the fancy suit was watching him. Not going to have anything to complain about to his bosses though.

Johnny and Gino were standing by the gate trying to look tough for these New York guys. Like maybe they looked tough enough these guys would come knock on their doors. Cast them in the big show.

But New York had enough mean mugs.

Mickey had been playing this role a long time. Long enough to know that. Maybe too long.

When the counting was all done and the big New York dudes had rolled the carts away from the time gate, the beady-eyed guy walked over and set the duffle bag of cash on the table.

"Mr. Amadeus appreciates your punctuality. We'll be in touch again when we have need of you."

"Our pleasure," Mickey said. "Anything he needs, we got it covered."

Beady-eyes twitched his lip, then snapped his fingers toward one of the dudes by the gate. The guy activated it. Mickey's cue to go. He picked up the bag of cash. Kept a smile on his face and pretended it was heavy enough to satisfy him. He went three feet and handed it to Johnny to carry. Johnny's eyes got big and he couldn't keep the stupid grin off his face.

The gate glowed bright.

Mickey took one last look at the New York guys. Nobody was even watching no more. Business concluded.

When he stepped back through the time gate to Bay City, he looked around his warehouse and sighed.

Place looked like a shithole after the high-end scene they just visited in Manhattan.

But maybe not for long.

He played this right, maybe he'd be in Maui on the beach next week. Let New York find another donkey for their dirty work.

Gino and Johnny had all the subtlety of drooling dogs the way they stood around that bag of cash. But well-trained dogs. They wouldn't touch it till he said so.

"Go ahead, boys. Open it up."

Time to celebrate.

Johnny and Gino dug into the bag, whooping and hollering. Started counting out stacks on the big table they'd used for the gold. Big pile was Mickey's. He didn't even have to tell them. They just laid it out. They knew their usual shares and split their meager ten percent. Goofy smiles on their faces the whole time.

They were all right these two. When the sorting was done, they stood back from the table. Respect being given.

Mickey liked that. He surveyed his pile. The other two looked tiny beside it but still a good haul for a day's work.

Mickey picked up a stack from the top of his pile, then another. One for each hand.

Custom was he'd tip a little extra if the guys did good work. These two waited. Good dogs.

Mickey looked at the two stacks. "You know what? We're going to do something different today." He slid the two stacks into the pockets at either side of his jacket.

The smiles on Johnny and Gino's faces faded. Grins replaced by concern. Had they messed up?

"I want you two to have *this* pile," Mickey said, gesturing to what was in front of him. "On account of you boys been real hard workers."

Johnny's eyes widened first. "You mean *that* whole pile?"

"Don't spend it all in one place."

"Holy shit," Gino muttered.

"I'm gonna go up to my office," Mickey said. "You boys divide this up square. Don't get greedy with each other."

"We won't, boss," Gino said and started grabbing stacks.

Johnny was still staring. Mind working.

It was a lot of cash. Understandable.

Mickey turned around. Started for his office.

"Hey, Mickey?"

He paused. Turned around.

"You're being real generous with us," Johnny said. "It okay with you I give some to Cassius's little sister? On account of some of this would have been his?"

Mickey waved a hand. "You do what you want with it. It's your money."

Johnny smiled broader. "All right. That's what I'll do then." He reached for the pile to start sorting again.

Mickey walked upstairs and unlocked his office door. The

two were still laughing and grinning when he stepped inside and closed it again.

Ought to be plenty to keep them occupied.

He went to the wall safe.

What the hell was that number again? He sighed, went to the desk drawer. Reached for the folded paper.

That's right.

This time when he opened the safe he found two Temprovibes inside. The frequency scanner. Another pistol too. His late doppelgänger's possessions.

He picked up the frequency analyzer and checked the last readout.

The other timeline was currently missing a Mickey Twitch. He could solve that problem.

New York was happy. None-the-wiser. They had their gold.

His boys had their payday.

It was time for Mickey to go get his.

CHAPTER 25

Greyson. 1995. Timeline 1.

"You're that guy. The kid from the other night with the gun. But grown up."

The man sitting across from me in the tavern was maybe fifty, polo shirt and khakis. He wore a gold watch that could drown him. Arrogant smirk. I'd seen that look on people's faces plenty. Entitled judgment. I didn't care.

"Let's keep talking about Heavens Archer. When was the last time you saw her?"

I had my notepad out. His name was Brad. Wife was Jean. They were on the tour from 2170. He'd mentioned his yacht twice so far. Jean had a headache and didn't want to talk to me, but Brad was enough talk for both of them.

"This is our fifth tour to the past. Never had to put up with something like this from the other companies. You can bet we'll be going back to Timeless after this. They have real security on their tours."

"You and your wife both went on the day trip to New

Orleans for the World's Fair visit. You remember the last time you saw Miss Archer on that excursion?"

"Shouldn't I be talking to a real time cop? If something is wrong, why don't we have TCID agents on it? It's what we pay their salaries for."

I consulted my notes. "A Donald Mather said you and your wives both ate at Le Bon Creole at noon. Miss Archer was in attendance?"

Brad grunted an acknowledgment.

"And this person?" I held up a photo on my phone.

He squinted. "Yeah, she was there."

Twenty more minutes and he didn't give me anything I hadn't already learned from the other dozen guests I'd interviewed. I'd been over the available security footage. It all confirmed roughly the same thing. Heavens and Sol had used the time gate to port the guests out for a day trip to New Orleans. Sol and the guests had returned via the gate, but no Heavens.

And one guest hadn't returned either.

The name she'd used on the roster was Nadia Frank.

Same woman who had chatted me up first night of the tour. I slipped on my meta lenses and studied the still shot I'd taken of her going through the time gate. She was looking right at the camera.

It wasn't a lot to go on. A face. A name. But Waldo had run facial recognition. And the few records he found pointed back to the 1980s.

Nadia Frank's real name was Nadia Roseland. She'd grown up in the foster system after the murder of her mother, a former prostitute. She had a half-brother. Cassius Roseland. Deceased. In some timelines.

This all came back to Cassius. To me.

To our history.

And I'd walked Heavens into danger.

The face looking back at me from the security footage was bold. Defiant.

She knew I would see her. Had he put her up to this?

If so, he knew I'd come looking. He'd be counting on it.

I tapped my earpiece. "Waldo. We have a problem."

"You think this woman has something to do with Heavens' disappearance."

"All the guests saw them together on the tour. Seemed like they'd made friends. Apparently hung out together. Till they didn't come back."

"Have you considered that something unfortunate befell the both of them?"

I studied the face looking up at the camera some more.

"No. This was planned."

"It seems you have insufficient evidence to make that assumption."

"I watch people for a living, Waldo. You do it long enough, it's easy to spot the truth."

"What motive would this woman have for inflicting harm on Miss Archer?"

The answer was simple enough. And excruciating.

"Because she found out I care about her. And it's payback."

"Do you think Cassius Roseland used Nadia Frank to get to you?"

"That's my first guess."

"Why would a person use another person as a means of inflicting pain on you?"

"Because humans suck as a species. And because I hurt them first."

I got up from my booth in the tavern and pushed my way through the door to the kitchen. Some of the kitchen staff watched me pass. I found Solena and Manuel in the back room that functioned as his office. They had been speaking quietly and both looked up as I entered.

"Well?" Sol asked.

Manuel crossed his arms.

"I'm going to bring her back," I said.

"You know where she is?" she asked.

"Not yet. But I have a few places to look."

"Do we need to call Time Crimes?"

"I got her into this. I'm going to get her out."

"This is about you?" Manuel spoke for the first time. "You make this mess?"

"Yeah. Looks like it. I don't think whoever is behind this wants to hurt Heavens. They're using her as bait to get to me."

"You go, she comes back?" Manuel asked.

"Something like that."

"Good trade," he said.

"No argument here."

He studied the doorway. "I'll come with you."

"I don't think that's a great idea."

"Maybe you screw it up by yourself."

"There is a chance this gets messy and Heavens wouldn't want me dragging you into it."

"She's in danger, so we go. She would expect that," Sol argued. "She'd do it for us."

I didn't doubt it, but dragging more potential victims into the situation wasn't on my to-do list.

"I need to find her first. When I do, if it looks like I need backup, I'll call you. I promise."

No doubt Solena and Manuel had the guts to walk into whatever trouble I was headed for, but I had enough blood on my hands. I didn't need to add theirs. And if there was going to be more, I also didn't want them getting in my way.

Luckily, they didn't fight me on it.

I headed upstairs to my room, but paused in the hallway.

There was something about the silence coming from the other side of Heavens' door that felt loud. Just knowing she wasn't in there made the whole building feel empty.

I opened the door to my room and walked in. It had only been a few days for me. Fewer here. But it felt longer. Even so, the room hadn't gone entirely unoccupied.

On the kitchenette table sat the small vase that had held the white rose I'd found in the hallway. The one I'd mistakenly thought had been left for Heavens. The stem was still in the vase but the top of the rose had been sliced off. The head of it lay on the table, wilted and losing petals.

It had been a threat. A warning.

One I'd missed.

Looking up old pictures of Cassius and his fighting days had revealed the logo too late. A white rose on the back of his sweatshirt. On his robe in the ring. A symbol pointing straight to him. It wasn't over between the two of us.

But it was going to be soon.

CHAPTER 26

Nadia. 1984. Timeline 2.

Nadia Roseland stared at the stack of hundred dollar bills on the table in front of her and tried to form words. She'd been in Johnny's apartment for nearly six hours. She'd cried for much of it. Stared at the walls for some. Even slept somehow. Maybe her body didn't know what to do with her. She'd read about how shock did strange things to people.

She'd thought about Cass the whole time. Even while dreaming.

Now this guy was back.

Johnny had a weird look on his face. Pride?

"I want you to have this. I think it's what Cassius would've wanted."

Five thousand dollars.

She could admit she'd never seen that much money in person before. But she'd seen plenty of movies. Certainly wasn't enough to have any feelings about it.

She stared back at Johnny. "But what about who killed him?

Your boss said he was going to find out who killed my brother. He said he has ways."

"He does."

"So when is he going to do it?"

Johnny ran a hand through his hair. "Look, I don't know when exactly, but soon, all right?"

"When is soon?"

"Soon soon. Like soon. Are you even looking at this right here?" He gestured to the money.

She looked. She looked at him too. What did he think, that because he had brought her this stack of bills that she would stop thinking about her brother getting murdered?

"Someone killed him," she said. "Who?"

"I don't know."

"You *said* you would help me."

"And I am. Look, I know this money is not like, fixing the fact that Cassius is gone, but maybe think of it as his last gift to you. And, you know, a gift from me too." He stood up and moved around the table, pulling a chair closer to hers. He sat and put an arm around her shoulder. "I told you I'm going to take care of you now. That's what I mean."

She felt the weight of his arm on her. A yoke. Maybe something else.

She knew what he meant. She was supposed to feel grateful. He was her knight in shining armor. She'd known guys like this. Got off on being a protector. Like he owned her now just because she was hurt. She *was* grateful. But she barely knew him. Had Cass even known him that long? She'd heard his name a few times. Seen him maybe once?

Now he was looking at her, holding her shoulder. He wasn't that old. Maybe twenty-two? All right looking too, even if he seemed to know it. But too old to be hanging all over her. What did he expect, she was going to look at that stack of money and get the urge to take her clothes off?

"Where did you get the money?"

"Job Cassius was planning to do with me today. Pretty big deal."

"And this boss of yours put you up to it?"

"Mickey? Sure. He takes care of everybody. I told you that."

"Didn't take care of Cass."

Johnny clenched his jaw. "Today was a bad situation. Unrelated to us. Came on a big day, but now we're done with this job, I'm sure Mickey will get to finding out whoever killed your brother."

"I want to see him again."

"Your brother?"

"Your boss. I want to talk to Mickey."

"He's busy."

"I don't care. I want to see him."

"Look, he just had this deal go down with these big shot guys in New York. Now we have the night off. We can go celebrate."

Nadia shrank away from him.

"I mean, not just celebrate. We had a good deal, but I know it's hard and all. Wouldn't Cass want you to make the most of it though? Let's get you out of here, get your mind off it." He tried to touch her shoulder again but she twisted in her chair.

"Will you take me to see Mickey or not?"

Johnny rubbed a hand over his face. "Okay. Okay sure. Real quick. We'll go by there. But if he ain't there, we're going to leave it alone till tomorrow, okay?"

Nadia rose, arms still crossed.

Johnny grabbed his keys.

Nadia took the money.

It was a short ride in Johnny's Oldsmobile. They passed a quickie mart on the way. Nadia got a weird feeling going by. Deja vu. Like she'd been there already tonight. She'd always hated that feeling. Like maybe she was doing something wrong. Going down the wrong path. Or forced to repeat it?

Today felt like a dream. Ever since she'd stepped off that bus. She wished she could wake up.

The old warehouse was past the train yard. When Johnny had brought her there earlier today, she hadn't even looked out the windows of the car. She'd been crying too much. Nothing much out to see anyway except the wrecks of old cars and the road to the city dump. Not what she imagined for a place of business.

The rusty sign on the warehouse said Salty Dog Shipping.

Twilight gave the building and sky a yellow sheen. She'd heard people call it the golden hour. Made sense here.

Johnny had keys to the place. Big warehouse, mostly empty but with a few trucks and shipping crates inside. A forklift.

A second-floor office level overlooked the warehouse space and a catwalk ran the perimeter and crossed at the midspan. Lights in the office were still on.

"We'll go up, see if he's there," Johnny said. "But if he's not, we take off. Got it?"

"What's that?" Nadia asked, pointing to a strange doorway erected on one side of the warehouse that seemed to go nowhere.

"Don't worry about that."

"What is it?"

"Nothing. Just something for work."

"You don't know?"

"'Course I know."

"Doesn't sound like it."

Johnny let out an exasperated sigh. "You think I don't know my own job? You wouldn't believe me if I told you. Things I know, nobody knows."

"So you're a big deal here at your job?"

"Better believe it."

"Then what is it?"

She couldn't put words to why she liked seeing him frustrated, but she did. She was mad and he was there and maybe that's all it was. But getting under his skin was easy and it let her feel something. Like she could move him. And it felt like she was doing something. Because she'd done nothing all day and she was done doing nothing. Cass was dead and somebody needed to pay for it. Right now it was Johnny.

Johnny pointed a finger at his chest. "I'm a top dog around here. One day I'll probably run this shit. You know what I made today? Guess."

"Ten dollars."

He gave her a smirk. "That stack I gave you? I got twenty of those."

"A hundred thousand dollars?"

"Bet your ass."

She shrugged. "I guess that's a lot."

"Damn straight it's a lot."

"You going to buy a nicer car?"

"Cars, big house, whatever I want. You're lucky and treat me right, maybe I'll let you see some of it."

She studied him. He was so easy to see through. Big talker who wanted her to be impressed. Trying to get in her pants. Did he have trouble talking to girls his own age or something? Seemed like the type who might. He did have that money though so he wasn't completely full of shit.

"Can you get more money?"

"Better believe it."

"How?"

"Easy. You just wish you knew."

She thought about what she would do if she had a hundred thousand dollars. Enough to buy her own place if she wasn't still sixteen. If Cass had been the one to get that money he could have gotten custody of her. Finally got her out of foster care. He wouldn't have spent all his time trying to get laid like this guy was. She could have been safe. They'd been so close.

Cassius should have been the one to get that money. She'd have traded a hundred Johnnies.

They walked upstairs. Johnny knocked. They waited.

"I don't think he's in there," Johnny said.

"Try the handle."

Johnny hesitated.

"I thought you were big shit."

He tried it. The door swung open.

The office was empty.

She wasn't sure what she expected. Pretty dull. She walked in. It was big. Had a cool fish tank at least. Multicolored lights and a little castle that bubbled. The fish looked tropical. There was an ugly print of a boat on the wall behind the desk. Maybe Mickey was trying for an island vibe.

"Let's bail," Johnny said.

Nadia walked around the broad oak desk and looked at it. Sat in the chair. Had Cass ever been in here? Mickey was his boss too, right?

Johnny lingered by the door. She was making him nervous. Good.

She studied the phone, opened a couple of drawers. Not much of a big shot boss. Just a bunch of papers.

"Get out of there. That's Micky's shit." Johnny took a step in.

"You said he's not here."

"He could come back any minute though. You never know. Not supposed to be in here."

"What, like he'll appear out of thin air? Relax."

She looked through some nonsense in the desk. Boring shipping invoices. But there was a folded slip of paper too.

Looked like it had been folded a bunch of times. Handwritten numbers on it. Reminded her of her locker combination at school the way it was written out.

"Let's go," Johnny said.

But she was having too much fun watching him sweat. He was like a nervous dog, easy to make whine. That's what he reminded her of. A whiny puppy. She swiveled in the office chair, taking in the bland furnishings. The ugly boat painting on the wall was crooked.

She stood up and walked to it. Took it down.

The wall safe was right there.

"Get out of there," Johnny said, entering the room finally.

"Thought you said you practically run things," Nadia said. "You know what's in here?"

"That's Mickey's shit."

"Like money?"

"Like whatever. Don't mess with it."

"You aren't curious what he keeps in here?"

He grabbed her arm. "Come on. We're leaving."

She held up the slip of paper with the numbers. "I have the combo. We can just take a peek. If Mickey gave you a *hundred thousand*, how much you think he has in here?"

Johnny stopped pulling on her arm. His eyes drifted from the paper to the keypad.

"Just a *tiny* quick look," Nadia pressed. "Then we go."

She put a hand gently to his face.

He caved.

This was too easy.

CHAPTER 27

Nadia. 1984. Timeline 2.

It wasn't just money.

Nadia and Johnny had opened the safe in Mickey's office. There were a few stacks of bills in there, but the item front and center looked like something out of Star Trek. Some kind of armband but fancy, with a glowing screen that lit up when you moved it. No buttons. You could press right on the screen. It was the coolest thing Nadia had ever seen.

Johnny was staring too.

"You know what this is?"

"Never seen one in person," he said. "Didn't know Mickey had one either."

She held it, mesmerized by the glow from the screen. Bunch of cool indicators and a logo that read *Temprovibe*.

"Does it play music or something?"

"Does a whole lot more than that." He had a new look in his eye. Temptation? But he took it from her and put it back.

There was a shiny revolver in there too.

"Okay. You seen what's in there. Happy?"

It was a stupid question. She was anything but happy. She had stepped into a new reality. One where Cassius was gone and the future she wanted had vanished. Going back to the group home tonight would be hell. They'd be looking for her soon. She'd already missed curfew. It wasn't the first time she'd run away. But she couldn't hide long at Cass's place. That was the first place they'd look.

Johnny checked his watch. "Shit. I'm supposed to be somewhere soon."

"Where?"

"Place you can't go."

"You're leaving me?"

He grimaced. "I don't want to. But I was supposed to take a big trip tonight."

"Out of town? Take me with you." The words were out of her mouth before she even thought about them. It wasn't that she wanted him to be the person she was stuck with, but she wasn't ready to be alone.

"Not that kind of trip."

There were things he wasn't telling her and it was infuriating.

"Look. I can't go home. I don't want to be by myself right now. And you said you'd help me."

Johnny had his wallet out. He was looking at some kind of card in it. "This place is real exclusive. I been planning to go for a while."

"And what, I'm not good enough for them?"

"Nah, it's not like that." He rubbed his jaw. "Shit. Did Cassius tell you anything about what we did with him? The . . . treatment?"

"No."

Johnny nodded. "Figured he'd keep it tight like he was supposed to."

"You going to tell me what the hell you're talking about then?

It have something to do with what's in there?" She pointed to the safe.

"Yeah, sorta."

She waited.

"Look. I'm not supposed to be telling people. It's like, the rules."

"I'm not an idiot. I know you don't make a hundred grand cash in a day doing things that are legal. I'm not going to narc on you if that's what you're worried about."

"It's a complicated situation."

"You promised you'd help me. I need you to help me. What's complicated about that?"

He stared at her.

For all his bravado and the gold chain, he wasn't nearly as tough as he wanted to be. She could tell he was caving. She put a hand on his arm, stroked it a little. "Please?"

He sighed.

"Look. You gotta swear not to tell nobody. Not a soul."

She nodded.

"Mickey will be pissed he finds out you said shit to anybody. Real pissed."

She crossed her heart. It seemed silly but he must have liked it.

He took her hand. "I'm going to tell you. But not here. What do you know about how time works?"

Thirty minutes later they were in his car, sitting out front of an all-night diner. Still talking. She wasn't sure how to believe anything he'd said.

Time travel?

He'd talked for a while. Names of things she'd never heard of. Weird science stuff and future technology. He'd showed her his "phone." It had the cool face like that machine in the safe had. One you just press and things happen. Said he'd bought it off one of the New York guys from the future. It didn't actually work to call anybody which was lame, but it took cool pictures and had a flashlight. He told her some things he knew about the future. Names of famous people and companies.

But she didn't care much about any of that. He'd answered her biggest question with a no.

"You can't change the past. You do, it messes all kinds of shit up."

Like going back and keeping Cass from getting killed.

He'd explained it but she still wasn't sure she understood. Parallel worlds? Alternate timelines? Time police?

All she knew was the world was different than what she thought. Regular people walking around just didn't know. Nobody did.

Johnny had explained that it was a whole secret society of time travelers. Most of them in the future.

Mickey Twitch was one. Johnny too. And Cass had made it in. Cass had been a *time traveler*.

They worked for some people in New York.

She had trouble believing at first, but the more he talked, the more it added up.

The way Johnny explained things sounded like he was leaving a lot out. Not on purpose, but there was a bunch he didn't know. But that made it more convincing too. He wasn't clever enough to make this story up.

She still had questions.

Where Mickey got that machine. How the special particles you needed really worked.

Johnny knew how to operate the gate they had in the warehouse, though. One that looked like a door to nowhere.

"How can you tell if someone is a time traveler?" Nadia asked.

"You don't, 'less you do a test. Look for the particles."

That part was frustrating. None of the machines worked unless you had the special treatment. Gravitites. Apparently Johnny had drunk a bunch of them and also been treated in a special machine they had at the warehouse. Cassius too.

It was all illegal.

You were supposed to go to some school in the future to be a time traveler. Or belong to an organization with a weird name Johnny said was a bunch of science nerds with big egos.

So even in this secret society there were levels. Sounded like Johnny was about as low on the totem pole as time travelers came, unless you counted Cass.

That meant *she* wasn't even in the club.

But she couldn't help thinking about it. The possibilities.

One thing was for sure. School didn't matter anymore. Stupid Kent at the group home didn't matter either. The cops would be looking for her, ready to drag her back there. But this could be a ticket out of all that. Cass had found it. Was he planning to take her with him?

She didn't understand all the rules and science but she knew she'd come too far to go home now.

She looked across the seat at her unlikely savior in his tracksuit, sitting behind the wheel watching her.

Sticking with him was a choice that would come with strings. She wasn't naive about that. But if this was all real—and Johnny "Fastball" McKee was a time traveler—she could become one too.

She was going to figure this out.

And when she did, whoever killed Cass was going to pay big.

CHAPTER 28

Greyson. 1984. Timeline 1

The address was an apartment block on a rundown street you wouldn't let your dog piss on.

I parked the Boss a half block away and watched the place for a bit. I'd have to get close eventually but that would be after nightfall. There were several other cars on the street. Mostly boxy four-door sedans. A Plymouth Gran Fury sat on blocks in someone's front yard with two wheels missing.

To pass the time I used the touchscreen feature of the Boss's windshield to identify more. Waldo pulled up specks on the cars that drove by and put them on the display screen. The smaller cars had names like Gremlin and Chevette. There were a few Beetles and one pretty good-looking Datsun 240Z. It idled near the far corner of the apartments and a chick with a mohawk and a lot of eyeliner came off a stoop to pass the driver something. They talked less than a minute before the Datsun drove off.

Mohawk Girl did a brisk business while I was there. There were a few other business-oriented individuals hanging around too, though some of their business was simply loitering and smoking while looking menacing. A kid on a skateboard stopped to admire the Boss. Then he pulled something sharp from his pocket and was about to gouge fun words in the paint till I opened the door and ran him off.

He flipped me the bird as he went.

Good to know some things stayed the same.

Twilight brought new arrivals. But they were few and far between. Most of the people only lingered around till the glow of televisions lured them indoors. *The Love Boat* wasn't going to watch itself.

It hadn't been difficult locating Cassius's old apartment from this decade. He had linear records here. Waldo did the heavy lifting, searching electric company bills and scouring for his address.

I didn't like revisiting this day. It was a shit day. Too much blood. All of it bad. But I needed more information and this was a place to start.

I checked the time. Waited.

"If you last spoke to Cassius in nineteen-ninety-eight, why are we back in nineteen-eighty-four?" Waldo asked.

"When he got out of prison, he came back to this timeline, then came after Heavens. Figure he put the sister up to it. But he said she died. I want to know if he's lying about anything else."

"How will this help you locate Miss Archer?"

"All my history with Cassius comes back here. It will tie back to this day somehow. And you'd be surprised how often someone's past is a roadmap to their future."

"Is this another of your 'gut' feelings?"

"Maybe. I'm not sure what to think of Cassius's story yet. Some people tell the truth and still don't tell *all* the truth. Or they lie but there's truth in there too. Before I go up against whatever I'm getting into, I want the whole picture."

"Miss Archer is in danger."

142

"And she'll be in more danger if I get things wrong. Situation like this, knowledge is the best weapon I've got."

It was well after dark when the Oldsmobile pulled up. Two men inside. Cassius was behind the wheel. Didn't know the guy in the passenger seat. He got out and said something. I used the touchscreen interface on the windshield again and zoomed. When the guy walked toward the apartment building, it was casual. Playing it cool.

This 1984 version of Cassius sat in the car. Dome light stayed off. I watched, he sat. Nothing much happened for twenty minutes.

The boredom must have cracked him first. He got out and stared at the building a bit, then made his mind up about something. He looked my way. He could probably see the Boss from there but he wouldn't be able to see details through the windshield. Still, he stared a little before locking up the Olds. He checked it twice then made his way toward the apartment building.

It turned something in my stomach seeing him this age again. Looked so young. When I'd shot him he'd been older than me. Now I was the one with the years. Felt different. Punching up, you feel like the hero. Take down someone bigger, older, wiser, you've earned something. Punch the other way and you're a bully. I had all the advantages on this kid now. But he was going to grow up too.

He went inside a place on the second floor. Same place as the first guy.

I watched some more.

After a few minutes a shiny Chrysler Town and Country cruised by. Nice car for this neighborhood. It slowed near the Olds, driver having a look. Who was this guy? But he drove on and turned the corner.

I climbed out of the Boss.

"Waldo, I'm going to take a closer look at what's going on up there. Pull the car behind the building and keep watch. You see anybody leave that way, get it on video."

"It goes without saying that we can't interfere with the events of this timeline," Waldo said.

"If it goes without saying, why'd you say it?"

"Sometimes you make decisions I don't understand. Especially when your heart rate is elevated the way it is now."

"If I could check your vital signs, what would they tell me?"

"That I'm a perfect and logical machine," he replied. "Obviously."

It got a smile out of me. "See you in a few, buddy."

I closed the car door and patted the hood. I made my way around the side of the apartment. Waldo used the electric drive to glide out of the parking space but when he got to the end of the block, he fired up the gas engine. In 1984 a Mustang needed to make a little noise.

I walked quietly.

There was a stairwell on the opposite side of the building from the one Cassius had climbed. I used that.

The upstairs walkway ran around the back side of the building but there was a second row of apartments backing up against the front. I hadn't seen a blueprint to the place but it looked like only one way in or out of each unit. Made my life easier.

I went back to the corner near the stairwell and lingered, listening. There were two apartments between my hiding place and the door Cassius went in. No closer hiding places. I had a micro camera in my wallet so I stuck that to a hallway railing and watched the corridor via my phone while I stayed out of sight.

When Cassius came out, he wasn't alone. He had a woman with him. Could that be the sister? Both had sweatshirt hoods up so I couldn't make out features on the woman but it was enough to know it wasn't a dude. They walked with hurried steps in the opposite direction. Down across litter-strewn weeds that stood for a lawn, then to the Oldsmobile. It came to life and lumbered off in a cloud of smoke, bumper nearly dragging on the ground.

Waldo pinged my phone. He'd spotted the car departing.

I texted back.

>>> SAW IT. GOING TO CHECK THE APARTMENT WHILE I'M HERE.

Waldo replied. <<< STILL ONE IN THERE.

I put away my phone and pulled my gun.

The place had a window that was probably a bedroom but the shades were down. Hallway lighting was minimal but I made sure not to let my shadow cross the blinds. Door had no window. Front room had one though and the blinds were missing a slat. I listened near the door first, then stooped to peer in the window. The lights were all off with the exception of one over the oven.

Front room was a kitchen/dining room.

If that dude was still in there, he was being quiet. Past the dining room was a tube TV. It was off. Not much else was in view.

I tried the doorknob. Locked.

It was a problem I had a solution for. But it required me putting away my gun first.

I pulled the lock pick set from my pocket and crouched at the knob.

A noisy couple walked the sidewalk out on the street but they didn't look my way. Took me about twelve seconds to get the door unlocked.

I had my gun back out when I turned the knob.

You have to use all your senses trespassing in a place for the first time. First one here was smell. Place had a bouquet of odors. Trash can near the door needed emptying. Dirty dishes in the sink. Somebody had tried mothballs recently. But that wasn't all.

145

Somewhere beyond the thrift store smell of old furniture and the damp of a ceiling leak was a scent that didn't belong. A metallic acidic tinge to the air.

Blood.

And it didn't take long to find.

There was a dead guy on the living room carpet.

CHAPTER 29

Mickey Twitch. 1984. Timeline 1.

His office looked the same.

Not sure why he thought it wouldn't, but Mickey didn't do a lot of traveling to alternate timelines. Everything was pretty much how he'd left it in his own time, which made sense, considering he'd only been duplicated since lunch. This other him had the same operation going on today, but where the hell was everybody?

He pressed the intercom on his desk.

"Hey, you got any calls for me?"

Claudia came back immediately. "Not since you asked me ten minutes ago. You getting edgy up there or somethin'?"

He checked the clock on the wall. Other Him from the restaurant said the job was going off no problems over here. Johnny and Cassius went to dig up the gold in the cemetery.

Once they were back, this would be easy.

Maybe he ought to drive out there, check on things. He hated cemeteries though. All those stiffs just laying under there. Gave him the creeps. New York had insisted on the location. And that's where the gold was hidden. Hard to argue that.

Still, it was getting late and Johnny and Cassius shoulda been back by now. He'd better check.

He still had his piece and his Temprovibe. He'd keep them on him for now. New York was happy. This should be smooth sailing, but it didn't hurt to be careful.

He didn't know how many people might know about the changes here. Sounded like nobody. But he'd have to clean things up, make sure it stayed that way. Would he have to shoot Claudia? He'd try to avoid that. She had a kid. But whatever.

Not that he relished having to pop Johnny or the new guy either, but things could easily get out of hand if too many people started snooping around time. At least it wouldn't take all day.

Another benefit of running a lean operation. When it was time to clean house, it took fewer bullets.

He found his car keys and made his way downstairs.

Claudia was in the office watching *Bosom Buddies* on the Zenith.

"Hey. I'm going out. Those boys get back, you tell them to stay right here, get me?"

Claudia waved a manicured hand but didn't look at him.

His Chrysler Town and Country was where he left it. Plush seats, roomy interior. When he started it up, the electronic voice chimed.

"Your door is ajar."

His door was ajar. He loved that. He closed it.

"Please fasten your seat belt."

"Sure thing, honey." He did.

"Thank you."

Cars that talked. He was living in the future. Soon they'd be driving themselves.

He pulled away from the warehouse and crossed the tracks. Night was falling. He'd better get busy.

It wasn't far to the cemetery.

Gate was open when he got there. He pulled through and up to the little groundskeeper shack where the security guy had an office. The guy came lumbering out, squinting in the headlights. Mickey pulled a five from his pocket. "Hey chief, you had some visitors today, some boys of mine. They get things sorted?"

Security guy shielded his eyes. "That you, Mr. Twitch?"

"Yeah. Couple a guys in an Olds were here. Getting a little work done. You help them out?" Mickey passed the guy the five.

Security guy took the cash, gave it a quick glance and shoved it in his pocket. "Yeah. Left a little bit ago. No problems."

"Nobody hassled them?"

"No, sir. Nobody at all. Had the place locked up while they were here. All good."

"Okay. How long ago they leave?"

Guy screwed up his face, checked his watch. "I dunno. Forty minutes? Maybe forty-five?"

"You're a prince, buddy." Mickey passed him another five. "Keep up the good work."

"Thanks, Mr. Twitch." He tipped his hat as he backed away.

Forty minutes.

Mickey located a payphone on a corner and dropped in a quarter.

Claudia picked up. "Salty Dog Shipping. How can I help you?"

"Them boys back yet?"

"Not yet, sweetie."

"They get there, you tell 'em to stay put. You got an address for the new guy?"

149

"Sure. You need Johnny's too?"

"Nah. I know where he lives."

She gave him the address for Cassius. It wasn't far. He'd have a look.

Maybe they stopped for a shower? It was dirty work.

He knocked a cigarette loose from his pack. Lit it and took a drag.

He coulda had more guys. But it was a lot of gold. Their eyes mighta got big looking at all that gold. More guys, more eyes. Two had been enough. Maybe they were feeling temptations.

But he was Mickey Twitch. Everyone knew not to mess with his shit. There were things you did and things you didn't do, and you never messed with a time traveler's payday.

If there was trouble it would have to be someone else. Locals? Cops?

Guys could sometimes get in trouble. But he'd made Johnny check that car ten times. No cop was going to pull it over for having a tag light out. Probably shoulda used one of the box trucks for the weight, but Johnny was sure he could get it all in the Olds. Less conspicuous. Said a box truck in a cemetery looked outta place. Guy had a point.

Johnny was a good kid. Not always the brightest bulb, but reliable where it counted.

Maybe the problem was with the new guy then.

Whatever it was he'd have to sort it quick.

He flicked his cigarette out the window and steered the Chrysler toward the address Claudia had given him.

When he found the street he cruised down it slow.

There it was.

The Olds was parked out front of an apartment building. He eased up, had a look. Just sitting there. Nobody in it. That how they were looking after his goddamn gold? He was going to have to have a word about that.

But maybe this was an opportunity too. He cruised around the corner and looked for a space. Only trouble with this car, needed a big spot.

He found something halfway around the block and put the thing in park.

This wasn't even his timeline. Maybe Johnny leaving that car unattended was his chance. He could get behind the wheel, drive off with the gold. Get it out of here himself?

But nah, he'd have to bust in a window. Been a long time since he'd jacked a car too. Could he get it started fast enough? When he was eighteen he coulda done it in two minutes. That was young guy shit though.

The hell was he thinking? He could just walk up to Johnny and say there was a change of plans. Make him give him the keys. Maybe get mad about them leaving the car unattended. Yeah, that could work.

A car came around the corner. Black Mustang, windows so dark you couldn't even see a driver. Paint shiny as a saint's halo in the streetlights. That was a hot car. He waited till it went by before he got out. He checked his piece was in his pocket. He kept a hand in there as he walked. This neighborhood was a little rough. Anybody came after his hubcaps they'd have another thing coming.

He'd just made it around the corner when he saw the pair walking out of the apartment. He put himself behind a tree to watch. That was Cassius. But that wasn't Johnny. Looked like some chick. Hang on. Wasn't that the same chick Johnny had come into his office with? The little sister. What the hell was *she* doing here?

Then he remembered this wasn't the same timeline. Different sister.

He waited.

Cassius and the girl got in the Olds and fired it up. He

considered walking into the street and waving them down but something was up. Where the hell was Johnny?

The Olds cruised past, riding low. Driving away with his gold.

He shoulda stayed in his Chrysler. He could have followed.

But this was okay. They wouldn't get far. He had the Temprovibe. He could probably jump back, catch up if he had to. He could figure this out. Nothing to sweat about just yet.

He stood there a minute, thinking.

Shit always got a little confusing days he went time traveling. Hard to keep it all straight.

On the day he came from, Cassius was dead in the street somewhere. Johnny and Gino had done the job. Here, Cassius was alive and driving off with the gold and his sister and no Johnny. Something didn't add up, and if Mickey wasn't careful he might run right into it.

Then he saw the dude slinking along the top floor of that apartment building. Tall guy. Too tall to be Johnny. Who was this?

It was dark up there but it was definitely somebody.

Guy stopped at the door midway along the apartments, crouched to peer in the windows. Was that Cassius's place? Must be.

Mickey watched while the guy broke in. Door closed behind him.

Who the hell was this guy?

He didn't know what to do. Some other player was involved here. Was this guy with New York? Was he getting played right now?

Maybe Cassius had stashed the gold up there. Was this guy after it?

He didn't know this mook but that meant the guy probably didn't know him either. He could walk up there, have a look.

Like hell if this dude was going to get away with any of his money.

So he walked to the stairs at the side of the apartment and climbed up, hand on the grip of the pistol in his pocket. Just walk up there. Element of surprise. This asshole wouldn't know what hit him.

He walked slower nearing the door. It had been left open a crack. He paused near it and listened.

"Hey Waldo, what are we looking at here? Give me the breakdown."

Mickey froze. Were there two guys in there?

The guy inside spoke again. "Run some analysis. See if we can ID this guy."

Whoever this Waldo was, he was either talking too quietly to hear or he was on the phone. Mickey suspected the latter. Was he a cop?

He eased up to the door. There was enough of a crack to see light. The kitchen. Phone was still on the hook. He pressed on the door with one finger. His other hand eased his gun from his pocket.

The door moved a fraction of an inch. Enough to get a glimpse of the living room. There was the tall guy, back to him, looking down at the floor. Didn't look like a cop but you couldn't tell these days.

Mickey leveled his gun at the guy's back.

Then he saw the body on the floor. Holy shit. Was that Johnny? Looked like him. What the hell happened in here?

He didn't know how the guy heard him, Mickey hadn't made a noise, but suddenly he spun around, a gun in his hand.

Shit.

Mickey lifted his gun to aim and squeezed off a shot, but the guy wasn't staying still. He dove low and fired back from behind the half wall that divided the kitchen and living room.

The bullet whizzed so close to his face he felt it go by. He backpedaled. Blasted another two shots toward the living room, then turned and ran.

Damn it. He sprinted toward the stairs and elevator. Had they been that far away before? Hallway felt like a mile. He spun around halfway down it, skidded in his loafers, and fired another shot toward the doorway just in case.

He was panting when he reached cover. He took a two handed grip and aimed down the hallway, waiting for this guy to stick his head out.

How many shots did he have left? Two? He glanced down at his revolver and felt in his pockets. All his extra loads were in the damned car.

Screw this.

Wasn't planning for no gun fight.

He ran.

He was puffing when he made it downstairs and around the front of the building and his feet hurt. Needed to quit those damned cigarettes.

Gun back in his pocket, he gave several glances back over his shoulder as he went. A few people were peeking out windows, watching the commotion, but no one was in his way. No sign from the apartment upstairs though.

He hustled to the corner. His Chrysler was only twenty yards away on the other side of the street.

He made it five and got hit by a car.

CHAPTER 30

Greyson. 1984. Timeline 1.

"I've just hit a man with the car," Waldo said in my ear. "You will want to get down here."

I was still in Cassius's apartment, gun aimed at the front door. I slowly lowered it. "He still alive?"

"He's getting back up. I didn't hit him that hard. Would you like me to hit him again?"

"No. Hang tight. Just keep an eye on him. I'll be right there."

I looked around the apartment one more time. I still didn't know the identity of the corpse on the floor but I had some pictures. All I knew was he was the same guy that showed up with Cassius in the Oldsmobile out front.

I slipped my smart lenses on and used my phone to select a feed from the Boss's cameras.

The guy who'd shot at me was back on his feet. He was swearing a lot and waving his gun at the car. Looked shaken though.

Waldo revved the engine and the guy jumped.

I couldn't help but crack a smile. I noted the time and took the shades back off.

Okay. Needed to think this through. Cassius came here with this dude on the floor. Guy went upstairs, then twenty minutes later Cassius went up and walked back out with the girl. Had to assume that was Nadia, the sister.

Why kill the guy he came here with?

Then another dude shows up at the apartment to take a shot at me. Was he here for me or was he after Cassius? Or was he wanting to kill the dead guy on the floor and Cassius beat him to it? A lot of possibilities there. The body had no ID. But I'd bet the guy downstairs knew who he was.

I walked out of the apartment and back the way I came, retrieving the camera I'd stashed in the hallway.

It was a bit of a walk around the corner and over to where the car had been parked.

The Boss wasn't there. Neither was the guy Waldo had hit with it.

But that wasn't a worry.

I tapped my earpiece. "Hey, Waldo, you have a jump time for me?"

A text came through on my phone with jump coordinates.

I walked to the spot it noted and found the jump location. Just a phone pole in a back alley out of sight of the street. I set my chronometer and made the jump, reappearing fifteen minutes earlier.

The Boss was idling next to me in the street. I walked to the driver's side and got in.

"Good evening, Waldo."

"Welcome back, sir. Your temporal frequency suggests you've arrived from our near future. Anything exciting happen?"

"I get shot at."

"Would you like me to act surprised?"

"That's not all though. We get to hit somebody with the car."

"On purpose?"

"Definitely."

"I do enjoy that. Humans make interesting expressions when they realize they are about to be run over."

"You're getting pretty good at it."

I shifted the car into drive and we cruised around the corner.

"May I presume we are going to run down the person who shot at you or will it be another unfortunate individual?"

"Shooter guy. Maybe five-nine, white dude, had on a sport coat, collar with wide lapels."

"A man fitting that description was crossing the street a few moments ago. I passed him on the way here. I likely have camera footage."

"Go ahead and see if you can ID him. Can't hurt to know who he is."

"If he's a local, he'll be hard to identify. Public records are all still paper and few will make it into the digital databases I'm able to access in the future."

"Makes sense why so many time traveling hoods like to operate pre-internet."

"Any clues as to why he shot at you?"

"Wrong place at the right time? There was a dead guy up there, guy that showed up with Cassius. But I have a lot of questions to ask this dude when we get done hitting him with the car."

We pulled around the corner and waited. Wasn't hard to get the timing right. I had the window cracked and heard the gunshots.

The first few were muffled, then a couple louder ones. Twenty seconds later the guy in the Tony Manero collar came hustling around the corner. He was busy looking over his shoulder and Waldo had the car in electric drive.

Bam.

He went down hard.

"About like that?" Waldo asked.

"I told you you were good. Call the version of me that's upstairs. Let him know you hit a guy with the car and that he needs to get down here."

Waldo made the call.

I listened in as the earlier me and Waldo conversed. By the time they wrapped up, the guy we hit was back on his feet. He pulled his gun and started waving it. Looked like a .38 special. Window tint was so dark he wouldn't be able to see me. Hard to make a shot, especially since he'd already fired four rounds. There was a good chance he only had one left in that gun. I switched the car into gas mode and revved the engine. The guy jumped. Looked like he was thinking of shooting but just kept the pistol aimed at the car as he walked around and climbed into a Chrysler Town and Country. He pulled the Chrysler back so far he rammed into the car behind him, then he pulled out into the street and tore past, narrowly avoiding the Boss.

"What now, sir?" Waldo asked.

"Let's follow him."

There was no use being subtle. The Chrysler driver certainly wasn't. He was driving angry, blasting past slower cars and swerving aggressively.

"Where are you going?"

I kept on his tail, dodging late night traffic and coursing through downtown. He checked his mirrors a lot. Seemed to be swearing too.

Finally he pulled over in the parking lot of a well-lit nightclub. There was a crowd outside milling about. He forced people out of his way with the big car and climbed out. He made a beeline for a payphone, shoving a woman aside and casting angry glances at the Boss the whole time. This guy was armed and there were too many bystanders around so I just waited him out. He finished his call and climbed back into the Chrysler. Several women gave him the finger as he left.

"Somehow I doubt he called the cops, Waldo."

We followed him back into traffic. Where was this dude headed?

He had been trying to lose me before, but now he'd settled down. Almost seemed like he wanted to keep me on his tail.

"His driving behavior has changed," Waldo said. "I recommend caution."

"I'm with you, buddy. Keep an eye out for other vehicles. He might have called in reinforcements."

He was certainly taking us somewhere. Maybe planning to lure us into a collision of some kind?

But as I was busy checking the rear view cameras, every warning light in the car lit up. A man had stepped into the road ahead with what appeared to be a rocket launcher. The back of the launcher lit up and the rocket headed straight for us.

CHAPTER 31

Mickey Twitch. 1984 Timeline 1.

Mickey was tired of this day not going to plan.

So far he'd had a bad lunch, had to shoot himself in a bathroom, and gave a boatload of gold to the guys in New York. Things should have turned around by now. He had imagined that at this point in his day he'd be reveling in having acquired his own fortune and be on his way to Mexico or Tahiti with it.

Instead, he had found Johnny dead, had a shootout with some stranger, got HIT BY A CAR, and was now being followed by this dickhead. When he pulled into the lot of the nightclub, he only had one desire. Get this day back on track. For that, he was going to need a bigger gun.

The crowd in the parking lot was all young degenerates, punks with weird hair and strange clothes. He shoved one out of the way to get to the payphone.

"Hey, who do you think you are?"

He glared at her.

Someone was liable to pull a switchblade in this crowd, but let them try. Mickey was in no mood to take their shit.

He picked up the phone and dropped in a quarter, then glanced back at the street. That black Mustang was still out there. He pulled out his wallet and found the card with the number he needed. He started pressing buttons. This was the tedious part. You needed the code for the time you were in and the year you were calling. You had to dial a local tachyon pulse transmitter first and then put in the number for the destination with your account code to bill the call. So much to screw up. But eventually the phone rang through.

He tried to remember this dealer's name. Something with a Z. Zipper? No. Zigzag. That was it. Where did people come up with these names?

She picked up.

"What do you need?"

"Guns. I need something big, right fucking now. I need a machine gun. Or maybe a grenade launcher. You got those?"

"Year you are in, short order, I can do the gun. Kalashnikov, or a Papasha with a drum mag. No grenades today. I do have a shoulder-mounted rocket launcher you can access."

"Rocket?" He glanced to the street again. "Yeah, gimme that. And the machine gun. Gimme all of it."

"Charge your account?"

"Yeah, yeah, whatever."

"Need your authorization code and location."

He gave it to her.

"Your current location doesn't work but I can drop it north by the interstate overpass."

He got the rest of the details and hung up.

Mr. Mustang was going to regret interfering.

Mickey stormed back to his Chrysler.

"Hello," the car said as he started the ignition. "Please fasten your seat belt."

"Oh, shut up."

161

He drove slower this time. He hadn't been able to lose the guy in the Mustang yet, but there was no need now. He was going to send him to the afterlife on a cloud. Mickey shrugged out of his jacket as he drove. He rolled up his sleeve and accessed the Temprovibe on his wrist. Guy was going to regret messing with a time traveler.

How would he work it? Mustang Guy probably wouldn't sit still while Mickey pulled a rocket launcher from the drop site, but he didn't have to get that far. Mickey could come back in time and pick this guy off. Hell, there was a spot right up there looked good. He'd pick up the guns, jump back in time, post up there and blow this guy away. If it worked, maybe he'd even see himself up here right now. Mickey leaned forward, peering over the wheel.

"I'd come out right around *there*."

And sure enough, there he was. Another him, the future him walking into the street with the rocket launcher leaned on his shoulder. Future him pulled one hand from the weapon long enough to give him a thumbs up.

"Yeah!" Mickey shouted. "Hell yeah. Torch that bastard!"

He grinned as he watched his future self hoist the launcher and take aim. Mickey glanced in the rear view and the Mustang was still coming.

"Eat shit, you bastard."

He wanted to stay and watch but made himself keep driving. The light was visible from the rocket though. He kept glancing at the rear view. A streak of smoke, then the explosion.

BOOM!

"Yeah!" Mickey shouted. Did he get him? Was it a hit? He twisted in his seat but couldn't make out the details. Something was sure as shit on fire back there.

The Chrysler clipped a trash can and he swerved to get back in the road.

"Ha!" he shouted, getting the car straightened out. "Okay, okay. Now we're getting somewhere." A sign on the side of the road showed the interstate overpass was just ahead. Mickey grinned. This day was going to turn out all right after all.

CHAPTER 32

Greyson. 1984. Timeline 1.

I've never swerved so hard in my life. We were onto the curb, and over the sidewalk when the rocket streaked past and impacted a parked vehicle down the street. It lit the night in orange and black as shadows formed and light flashed. A fireball erupted upward like a dragon birthed into the sky.

The Boss was inches from a barbershop's front window. Everything glowed orange in the reflection. I shifted into reverse and punched the gas. I kept it on the sidewalk till I'd almost reached the exploded van, then cut the Boss back into the street again and spun around as fast as I could manage. The rear tires squealed as I raced away from the guy with the rocket launcher.

Rocket launchers win. Not worth even arguing.

I checked the rear-facing camera. Couldn't see the guy anymore. Who knew if he was reloading or had a second launcher.

The sparse traffic in the street was stopped and some cars were backing away. Didn't look like anyone had been injured, but vehicles around the van had taken a beating. Smoke billowed from the wreck in a choking cloud. I didn't linger, turning at the first available street.

"Emergency jump location?" I asked Waldo, scanning the road ahead.

"Data is limited here but there is a jump location with ninety-seven percent safety probability in four hundred feet." Using the windshield heads-up display, he lit the spot in the street ahead that would get us safely to another time.

There was a chance that anywhere we jumped from could be safe on landing, but we also could end up fused into another vehicle upon arrival. Travel by wormhole always seems like a great way out of a bad situation until you die painfully at the other end. I focused on the road ahead.

Then I saw the Chrysler pull into the street farther along. It was the same dude we'd been following.

He looked like something out of a Bond movie. Well-dressed guy with a nice car stepping out of the vehicle and lifting the rocket launcher to his shoulder.

Cars lined both sides of the street here. Nowhere to swerve.

I swore instead.

Three hundred feet to the jump location. I depressed the accelerator to the floor. The Boss's engine snarled and the car leapt forward.

"This seems counterintuitive," Waldo said.

Rocket launcher guy had his weapon loaded. He took aim.

My speedometer read 65 and climbing. Another second . . . 74 . . . 88. An absurd memory of childhood math classes flashed through my head, but instead of trains departing stations I had a car and a rocket launcher. If I was accelerating through sixty feet per second now, and needed to travel two hundred more feet to not be incinerated by a rocket launcher, how fast did the car need to achieve top speed before impact?

I had no idea what the answer was. Waldo likely did, but he

wasn't saying anything. When the back of the launcher bloomed with light and smoke, I'd already deployed the spacial anchor and my finger was on the jump button. A rooster tail of sparks glowed from the back of the Boss and the rocket flew straight at us, closing the distance in terrifying speed. I mashed the jump button and time seemed to slow, the tip of that rocket growing large in my windshield.

Then it was gone. The car reappeared twenty-four hours in the past, and I immediately wrenched the wheel to avoid plowing into the back of a pickup truck. I was into the oncoming lane then and had to swerve back in front of the pickup, just dodging a station wagon coming at me. Horns blared and headlights flashed. Everyone was angry.

So was I.

I pulled off the road at the next intersection and drifted to a stop at the curb of a quiet residential street.

"Holy hell, Waldo. That was close."

"Our demise seemed imminent," he said.

"I need to know who this guy is."

"Yet, I'd like to request avoiding him for the time being. At least until you back me up somewhere other than this vehicle's hard drive."

"Made you sweat too, huh?"

"I wasn't designed to reflect on my own impermanence, Greyson, but you continue to find ways to make me aware of it."

"Feeling a little impermanent myself right now. But we're alive. Going to take more than a rocket launcher to slow us down."

"Despite our narrow escape, we're no closer to rescuing Miss Archer."

"True. We still need to figure out where in the hell Cassius has her."

"You're still convinced he's the abductor."

"Revenge is a strong motive, Waldo."

"Fourteen years does seem adequate time to plan."

"If he's hurt her, he's going to wish he was back in prison."

"As a time traveler, I would assume you've planned to arrive before anything unfortunate can befall her."

"That's why I need to get the timing right. Get enough to go on about her circumstances without learning too much of the future that I mess it up." I shifted the car into drive again and got back on the road, searching the nav computer for our next destination as I drove.

"We do know Heavens was last seen with Nadia Roseland."

"She makes the perfect accomplice. And we already know Cassius lied about her being dead. I think I need to pay him another visit in 1998 and see what else he lied about."

"The gentleman with the rocket launcher was in two places at once during our pursuit. All evidence suggests he is a time traveler. Do you feel adequately prepared to confront another time traveler?"

"He definitely complicates things."

"It's possible he's also in pursuit of Cassius Roseland."

"It's an extra level of complication, but that's it. If he's involved in Heavens' abduction, he'll go down too."

"Your confidence despite any defined plan is less than reassuring."

The Boss's engine growled in response to my pressure on the accelerator. "I always have a plan, Waldo. We get there first."

CHAPTER 33

Mickey Twitch. 1984. Timeline 1.

Mickey Twitch stood watching the fire blooming down the street until the police sirens got too close to ignore. Then he grudgingly tossed the rocket launcher to the curb and walked away from it.

He hadn't expected that car to vanish right in front of the damned rocket.

Who expects a whole car to travel through time? Had to admit it was pretty cool though. They ought to make a movie about something like that. That would be fun. Except in the movie, Mickey could be the guy driving the car.

He checked his Temprovibe. Time to get out of here. Back to the car. Back to the future. He selected the coordinates in his return menu. Had to get out of here before this new time traveler opted for some payback.

He didn't like that this Mustang guy was a time traveler too. Gonna make his life complicated. If this guy was after the gold too, that could be a big problem.

Mickey made the jump back to when he'd left the Chrysler and immediately walked to the trunk. He opened it and viewed the contents. He was out of rockets. Still had guns though. That dealer chick had come through with a Kalashnikov and plenty of extra mags. He'd see how well this time traveler could dodge a machine gun. He hoisted the weapon in both hands and tried aiming at a nearby tree. God this thing was heavy. He'd never fired one before. What if it jammed?

Had to admit it looked cool. He felt better with his revolver though. It was small but he knew how to use it. What was better, the big gun or the one he knew would work?

He already knew the answer.

But it meant he had an extra gun. Maybe he'd wear the big one on his back like John Rambo. Now that was a great film. But it felt weird slinging a gun over his back. Kept wanting to swing around and get in his way. Strap was probably too long.

No. He needed something else. Another guy to hold the big gun and intimidate people so he could still get the effect. Johnny was dead in this timeline. Maybe Gino was still around. He'd be none-the-wiser, would he? The other Mickey had said he'd done the New York job with just Cassius and Johnny. Gino was probably drinking beer somewhere. Yeah, that would even things up a little. See how Mr. Mustang liked going up against two time travelers with guns.

Then Mickey would take that car.

He liked that plan even better.

Missing that car with the rocket might have been the best thing he could have done. When he got his hands on that time traveling Mustang, he'd have something to put the gold in.

He'd have the gold, he'd have the car, then New York could kiss his ass. He'd be so far gone they'd never see a hair of him.

Mickey climbed into the Chrysler and started the engine.

"A door is ajar," the car said.

"Better talk nicer to me, honey. You're gonna be put out to pasture."

He closed his door and pulled away.

Mickey rubbed his ear. Firing that rocket launcher had been loud as hell. Fun, though. Not his average day at the warehouse, that's for sure. He was off the map now and headed for the kind of night you only get once in a long while. He was going to change his future tonight. He'd get a drink when he found Gino. Something good to fire him up, give him the edge he needed. Maybe Gino would have a little coke on him. That could work too.

The neon lights of downtown glittered across his windshield. It was nights like this that made him feel alive. He was going to find Cassius, was gonna find that Mustang guy. Going to send them both to hell in a wave of lead. Maybe he'd pick up Claudia after. He always liked a little bit of Claudia when his blood was up.

Yeah. Tonight was going to be a good night.

CHAPTER 34

Greyson. 1998. Timeline 1.

The Cassius Roseland from his original timeline was living in an apartment close to the boxing gym. Figured he walked there when he went. He worked close by too, at a greenhouse, loading trucks with shrubs and watering plants. I staked out the place for an hour till he left, then beat him home by way of time travel.

The lock on his door wasn't hard to pick.

I waited inside in the dark.

He came home with a paper bag of groceries in his hand, shut the door and flipped the latch. He'd just pulled a six pack from the bag and set it on the kitchen counter when I stepped from the neighboring hallway into the light.

"Oh hell no," he muttered. "You scared the shit out of me."

I crossed the space in three long steps and slammed him up against the fridge.

"Where is she?"

"Hey, don't touch me, man."

I shoved again. "Where is she?"

"You better get your hands off me."

"Think I'm playing?" I pulled my Stinger and pressed the muzzle against his temple. "Where is she?"

He spoke through gritted teeth. "Pretty tough with a gun in your hand, huh?"

"You think this is all you should be scared of, you've got it wrong."

We glared at each other. Fourteen years of hate still there.

"Put it away if you think you're so bad."

Yeah. What the hell.

I took one step back, then tossed the pistol to the counter near the microwave. Shrugged out of my jacket.

He was on me in a flash. Right jab at my face. I barely got out of the way. But it was mostly a feint to get me with his left. He connected with my ribs and moved me back another foot. But I still had my jacket in my hands. I used it to bind up his next punch, and while he was busy getting his arm free, I hit him hard across his face. He reeled back a step. My hands were up now, elbows in. He wouldn't get another freebie.

He tossed my jacket aside and smiled. He closed on me. I swung. He turned and I connected with his shoulder. His fists came fast and angry, but I wasn't going anywhere now. We had lefts up to block and traded rights, both connecting with each other's faces, recoiling, swinging again. The kitchen was tight. We ricocheted off the appliances.

The room was all meaty thumps and fast breathing, nothing clean about any of the shots we were taking.

I was in a corner so I went at him, shoving hard and putting my whole weight into him. We both knocked into the flimsy dining room table and Cassius groaned as it jabbed him in the hip. I kept pushing and he went up and over, rolling away. Back on his feet on the other side, he picked up a chair and hurled it at me. It bounced off my upraised arm but was enough of a distraction that he was on me again, fist in my gut, getting some of the wind out of me. I wrestled him, using my height advantage to keep him bound up while he tried to twist and hit my ribs. We slammed into the wall shaking dishes in the nearby cabinets. He pushed away and swung again, got me in the face, then my left shoulder.

I tasted blood. Couldn't have said when my mouth had started bleeding. His knuckles were bloody too. Maybe that's what I was tasting. Who knew.

We were both breathing hard.

"This how you thought it would go?" he panted. "Or you need me to whip your ass some more?"

"Waiting for you to start."

He clenched his jaw and came at me again. We traded blows into the living room now, but it wasn't much more space. On the way he picked up a phone book and threw it at me. I caught it and hurled it back. I missed.

And it was all punches and elbows again, not even blocking this time, just trading shots, hammering each other as hard as we could. He hit like a truck. My whole upper body was flaring with heat and pain. We knocked a lamp over. It gave a weird, up-lit glow to our fight.

Our knuckles left bloody smears on each other's shirts and faces.

Might have only been a minute or two since we'd started but we were both breathing hard when we broke away from each other again.

Both still standing. I was bigger but he was faster. Neither was enough of an advantage.

We worked to catch our breath.

"I don't know why the fuck you're here," he panted. "But I spent a lot of time ready to end this. How long you want to go?"

My fists were still raised but they were lead weights. My shoulders were on fire. I took a step back and lowered my hands.

"Tell me what I want to know. Maybe I'll go. Otherwise we keep at this."

"I got no idea what you're even talking about." He lowered his hands too. Flexed his fingers. "Something about a girl?"

"Heavens Archer. From the Rose 'n Bridge."

He squinted. "That tall blonde bartender? From the night I got shot?"

"Yeah."

"What's this got to do with her?"

"You telling me you don't know? She's gone. You took her."

"The hell would I want to hurt her for? She probably saved my life that night. I was bleeding all over."

I frowned. "What's with the rose then? Why'd you lie to me about your sister?"

His eyes narrowed. "My sister? I didn't lie about nothing to do with her."

"You said she was dead. Killed in a car crash at eighteen."

"Because she was. You need to see the grave? Couldn't get out to be with her, remember? I left her by the side of the road that night and never got back to her because you fucking shot me. You got any more painful shit you want to bring up?"

"Your sister was at the Rose 'n Bridge on the '84 tour a couple nights ago. Older than eighteen. Figured you put her up to it."

"My *sister* is dead."

I was getting my air back. Heart rate coming down. Clarity coming with it.

It was a different version of his sister. One from the second timeline. Had to be.

That meant Cassius had nothing to do with it.

"Shit. This is my fault," I said. "I had it all wrong." I wiped a knuckle under my nose and it came away bloody. I stared at the wall, then down at my knuckle again before looking back to Cassius. "You got a towel?"

He sighed, shoulders finally relaxing, then moved to the kitchen. He grabbed a paper towel roll, tore a couple off, then tossed the roll to me.

We both stood there wiping blood off our faces.

He paused long enough to focus on me. "You telling me that Nadia is alive?"

I walked to his kitchen trash can and dropped a bloody wad of paper towels in. "Yeah. Sort of. A different version of her. You aren't the only one of you I shot."

"Say that again?"

"After I shot you at the Rose 'n Bridge, I went back in time, to before you killed my sister, and I put another bullet in you. Behind the K-Mart."

"Shit. The K-Mart? Oh yeah. Walked by there to get lunch that day. Day of the big job. You *killed* me?"

"Yeah. Before you could do any of it."

"Damn, man. That's messed up. Nadia was coming over that day. She see you?"

"I didn't know you had a sister at the time. Didn't care. I wasn't really thinking about much. I was a bit . . . reactionary."

"So you've shot me *twice* now."

"You killed my sister."

"Yeah. But you shot me before I even did it?" He mulled that over. "You couldn'ta done something else to stop things from going down that way?"

"Didn't want to. Wanted to shoot you."

He wiped more blood from his nose. "Thought that kind of thing was illegal. Changing the past."

"It is if you get caught."

He nodded, set his bloody paper towels on the counter. "Guess we *both* kinda assholes, huh?"

"Yeah. Guess so."

We stared at each other for a few long seconds. Then he

walked over to the counter by the fridge and pulled a beer from the six pack. He looked back for a second, then pulled another one and offered it to me.

I put out my hands and he tossed it.

I popped the top and we both drank at the same time.

It was still cold.

Only tasted a little like blood.

CHAPTER 35

Greyson. 1998. Timeline 1.

Cassius and I had finished the beers and I'd given him an abbreviated run down of the events from the tavern. The apartment was still a wreck but I'd picked up the chair he'd thrown at me earlier and was now sitting in it. He had the other one.

"I still don't think my sister would abduct anybody," he said.

"She had the motive and the opportunity. She left with Heavens and they didn't come back. Unless someone proves otherwise, she's my prime suspect. When was the last time you saw her?"

"Been a long time. She was just a kid."

"She grew up."

"You planning to call the time cops on her?"

"Maybe, if it comes to it. But I'd just as soon resolve it myself. She expects me to come. I assume it's why she's doing this."

He crossed his arms. "Best plan on me coming along then."

"Like hell."

"You think I'm going to let you walk out of here and go hunting my baby sister without me being there, you're crazy."

"I work alone."

"If by 'work,' you mean you go around shooting people, then I agree. More reason I'm coming along. Keep you from poppin' everybody you run into on the way there."

I frowned. "You and I don't exactly have a trust-based relationship."

He glared at me. "Oh, I know that. But if you try to ditch me, I'll get there anyway somehow, even it takes me all my life. You better believe I'm showing up. Besides, if Nadia did do this thing you said she did, who you think she's going to listen to, me or you?"

He had a point.

I stood. "Just because we aren't trying to kill each other this instant, doesn't make us friends."

"I can kick your ass some more after, if that's what you want."

I walked to the kitchen counter and picked up my gun. I slid it into my hip holster. "Okay. Where would Nadia have gone? There someplace special to you two she would have wanted to go?"

"Maybe. I'll have to think on it."

"Think fast. I'm getting a move on. If you're coming, grab what you need and meet me outside."

I walked out.

Moving quickly was the only way I wouldn't have time to second guess the decision.

A few minutes later, Cassius opened the passenger side of the Boss and climbed in. He tossed a bag in the back. Didn't appear to have a gun.

"Damn. This is a nice ride."

"Gets the job done."

"Greyson, Cassius Roseland is in our passenger seat," Waldo said through the stereo system.

I started the Boss's gas engine and turned on the temporal navigation system. "Thanks, Waldo. I'm aware."

"Your car talks?" Cassius said, closing his door. "This some regular Knight Rider shit."

"Less helpful than you'd think some days," I said. "It's getting him to shut up that's magic."

"Your guest already has better manners than you," Waldo said. "Maybe he has a job for an AI I can apply for."

"Even your car knows you an asshole, huh?"

"What's that saying? Takes one to know one?"

"Yeah. Good for us. Car fulla assholes."

I rested a hand on the shifter that also contained the jump button. "Where are we going, Cassius? If you're Nadia and your brother got shot, where would you go?"

"If the cops got involved, they'd have taken her back to the group home. She hated it, but it was where they were keeping her."

"So we start there?"

"If she was over eighteen when you saw her, there's no way she'd still be living there now. Woulda aged out. But maybe they know something about where she is."

"All right. It's a start."

Waldo handled the jump across timelines and back to early 1988. This was the timeline where Nadia had grown up without a brother and if we were going to find answers, it would be here. Cassius took the time travel in stride, watching the scenery around us vanish and the trees get shorter, but I could tell he was impressed.

I was just guessing at a date based on how old Nadia would

have been when she aged out of foster care, and how she looked when I'd seen her at the Rose 'n Bridge. We had to start somewhere.

When we got to the approximate year, we drove it old school, cruised the streets till we found the foster home. It was an old Victorian house with peeling paint and a rusty jungle gym visible in the backyard. We had to wait for two kids on Big Wheels to roll past on the sidewalk before we could get to the house. Not sure who they belonged to. The kids just kept going.

Cassius had his hands in his hoodie pockets. "Always hated this place."

"You stayed here?"

"Not long. I was almost grown when my mom died. Nadia's the one got stuck."

We crossed a lawn of browning St. Augustine grass to the front porch and climbed the steps. The front door was open with just a screen door barring access. Somewhere inside, a TV was on. I pressed the doorbell and nothing happened so I knocked on the doorframe instead.

"They never hear anything," Cassius said. He opened the screen door and walked in.

Security in '88 was a little lacking.

There were two grade-schoolers watching She-Ra on the couch in the living room we passed. They barely looked up.

Cassius led the way down the hall to a room made up as an office. There was a dumpy, middle-aged white guy in there on the phone, cord wrapped around his hand. He looked up and his eyes widened at the sight of Cassius.

"Look, hey, I gotta call you back. Yeah. Shit never stops around here. All right, later."

He set the handset back and untangled himself from the cord. The desk had swear words scratched into it on the side facing us and one anatomically dubious sketch of men's genitals that had been ineffectively scratched out. .

The guy stood. "Hey, I . . . know you, right?"

"What's up, Kent," Cassius replied.

"You look like . . . Cassius?"

"Yeah, it's me."

"Holy shit. Aren't you supposed to be dead? They told me you were dead."

"Not dead. Where's Nadia?"

"You look *grown up*, man. You got like, older."

"Nadia, Kent. Where she at?"

Kent was having trouble processing things. Happened a lot when meeting time travelers.

"Kent, I'm Greyson Travers, a private investigator." I flashed my badge. Sometimes it snapped people out of a fog. "Mister Roseland here is interested in locating his sister. Can you help us out?"

Kent dragged his eyes from Cassius to me and it seemed to aid his focus. "Uh, yeah, Nadia bailed out of here years ago." His eyes drifted back to Cassius.

"Stick with me here, Kent," I said. "Where did she go?"

"Go? Hell, man, totally off the map for a bit. We looked, you know. Truancy was all over us trying to locate her. Social services. But runaways are runaways. We get it a lot."

"When was the last time you saw Nadia?"

"Day she ran off, I guess. Day he . . ." he couldn't help looking at Cassius. "Day, uh, they told me *he* was dead."

"She have any good friends here, somebody she might have stayed close with?"

He put up his hands.

Real helpful, this Kent.

Cassius was staring hard at him. So much that Kent couldn't

help but shrink away. He was leaning back so far he looked in danger of falling over.

"I want you to know something, Kent," Cassius said, taking a step closer. "You was always a real piece of shit to Nadia. You should be fired from this job. You was always a sonofabitch to me too. But I forgive you."

Kent blinked. "What?"

"I *forgive* you, Kent."

Kent looked back to me, unsure. I didn't have anything for him. I was as confused as he was.

I put a business card on the man's desk. "You think of anything about where we can find Nadia, you give me a call, okay?"

Cassius was already walking out. I turned to follow.

I was almost to the door when Kent spoke again. "Hey, Cassius?"

Cassius turned.

"I'm, uh, glad you're not dead."

"Thanks."

"And hey, I don't know if it's anything, but I heard a rumor, for what it's worth, maybe six months ago. Kids claimed Nadia was living on the East Side, living with some guy."

"East Side," Cassius replied.

"You know how these kids talk. Half of everything they say is bullshit. They also say she's a big shot drug dealer or something too, and drives a Trans-Am. Probably nonsense."

"This guy she's living with have a name?" I asked.

"Not sure of his real name," Kent said. "Kids just called him Fastball."

Cassius and I shared a glance.

"Thanks, Kent," I said.

I waited till we were back on the front porch and the screen door had slammed shut before I spoke. "You know somebody named Fastball?"

"This day keeps getting weirder, man. I don't think I like it."

"First time in an alternate reality is hard. You'll get used to it. Your forgiveness gimmick worked like a charm in there, though. Nice move."

"Ain't a gimmick, man. I meant it. Been hanging on to a lot of hate for that man. Time to let it go." Cassius looked up at the overcast sky and exhaled. Then he looked to me. "Not for nothing, but you look like you carry a lot around too. You learn to set it down, you get lighter. Lighter all the way down to your toes."

"You wanting me to forgive you? That what you're fishing for?"

"Nah, man. I'm not asking for nothing from you. I already took enough. Just letting you know how I see things now." He walked off the steps and headed for the car.

It took me a second to follow. When I did, I was still moving slow.

CHAPTER 36

Nadia. 1987. Timeline 2.

Nadia Roseland sipped coffee with the hand that wasn't holding the gun.

This would be the night.

Heavens Archer was bound in a chair across from her, looking tired.

It *had* been a long day.

Nadia had underestimated the mental energy required in hostage taking. Johnny may have done the bulk of the physical labor, but this was Nadia's plan. So far, it had gone flawlessly. No one had suspected them.

And as far as hostages go, this one was proving manageable. Nadia appreciated that Heavens hadn't spent a lot of time whining or pleading or making idle threats.

If anything, Nadia would have liked her to talk more. Kill some of the time.

Johnny was on guard. They had a few locals on patrol of the warehouse too. A sniper on the roof. Didn't hurt to have more guns when they were up against a time traveler.

"How long you think he'll drag this out?" Nadia asked. "Surprised he's not here by now."

Heavens lifted her head and straightened. "I suppose he'll come when he's ready."

"You don't seem as worried as I'd expected. You been held hostage before?"

"No. First time."

Nadia sipped her coffee again. "How is it going for you so far?"

"Could use a more comfortable chair."

"The guys suggested tying you to the pull-out bed in the downstairs office, but I didn't like that. Too rapey. Didn't trust that they'd leave you alone."

"I'm grateful then."

"It wasn't all bullshit. I did enjoy our friendship on the tour. The bar, New Orleans. All of it. You're good at what you do. It's nice seeing another woman in charge of things, especially that tavern."

"You seem to do all right in control yourself."

Nadia shrugged. "Took a few years, but men are easy to figure out. Johnny needed some direction. Turns out I gave him that."

"You run this crew now?"

"It's a partnership, technically." She glanced out the office window to the catwalk where Johnny was surveying the warehouse. "I wouldn't tell Johnny he's not in charge anymore. And to be fair, there are some kinds of men who only want to listen to other men. I can say the exact same words and it's like they don't hear it. You deal with that crap at your job too?"

Heavens shifted in her seat and stretched her neck. "It gets a little better in the future. Every generation you pass raises kids that are a little less chauvinistic. Takes a while to make up for centuries of it, though."

"I'd like to see more of that kind of future. Maybe when all this is done."

"You had to have seen some of the future if you found me. You figured out how to find Greyson."

"Yeah, but it took longer than I thought. I thought once I had that time machine it would be easy. A nearly infinite multiverse? That blew my mind a little, I'll be honest."

Heavens didn't look scared. She looked patient. Would have been nice to have her on her side during all this. Nadia could have used a friend like her. Someone who got what it was like to be a woman with a plan. Would have made the time travel a lot easier, that's for sure.

"They trained you, I bet," Nadia said. "How to be a time traveler. Johnny said there's a school, and lots of rules to learn."

Heavens nodded.

"That where you met your boyfriend?"

"Greyson isn't my boyfriend. And he didn't go to school. He was born a time traveler."

"You seem pretty confident he'll come through for you, even though you say he's not your boyfriend."

"Some people are a certain way. They do what they do no matter what you say. They're just . . . inevitable. That's what Greyson is like. That's why he'll come."

"I've seen the way you look at each other. He wants you. Maybe he's only showing up because he wants to get in your pants."

"If that was all he wanted, he could have found a way by now."

Nadia laughed. "Aren't you the slutty one."

Heavens sighed. "When you get a little older, you'll probably understand. You're a beautiful girl and I'm sure there are plenty of guys who have wanted to sleep with you just for that reason alone. Maybe you've used it to your advantage. That's fine. A little casual sex might be good for some people. But there are other people who are life-altering. You meet them and time changes. Whatever path you were on before is going to be different now because you've collided and there's no going back to who you were before. Part of you will always be different. Sometimes you know as soon as you meet them. The rest is just waiting to see what that new path will look like."

"Wow. That's some inspiring bullshit. Almost makes me sad I have to kill him and ruin the illusion for you."

"You have to try, I suppose."

"It's silly if you think *destiny* is going to save him for you. I may not run a time-traveling bar, but I know that better than you. Destiny doesn't save the people you love. Everybody can die. Even the people who matter the most to you in the whole world. So I'll make my own path. I don't wait around for destiny."

"Good for you." Heavens met her gaze and didn't look away.

Nadia stood. "Be smug if you want. You'll be less smug when he's dead."

She walked to the window and fidgeted with the pistol in her hand again.

He just needed to get here already. She checked the room again, kicked a chair a few inches to the right. They'd already moved everything in the room, changed the layout continually, making it harder for a time traveler to jump in from another time without killing themselves. There wasn't a single space in here that had been the same space yesterday. They had cameras, armed men in the warehouse. They weren't supposed to kill Travers though. That was her job.

Now they just needed him to show up.

Nadia glanced at the Temprovibe on her arm. It was set and ready. When Greyson Travers arrived, he'd have a short visit. She'd make sure of it.

CHAPTER 37

Greyson. 1988. Timeline 2.

Cassius and I were cruising the streets on the east side of the city without much of a destination. I was missing vital pieces of the puzzle we needed and Cassius knew it.

"This what you detectives do? Just drive around and hope shit falls in your lap?"

"Sometimes," I admitted. "I think better when I'm driving."

"Fancy car and time traveling watch and all that, I figured you'd have this all figured out."

"I'll tell you a secret about the future. There's no substitute for thinking something through. No matter which decade you live in or technology they come up with to save you time, it's never enough. People always think life will become easier in the future and it doesn't. All we ever get is right now and if you can't figure out how to use your right now to get things done, no amount of tricks or hacks can do it for you. And sometimes what you need to do with your right now is just sit and think."

"Had plenty of time to sit and think in prison. But I hear you. Since I been out it's been harder. People all about having the TV on all the time and the Internet hooked up and they ain't even invented smartphones here yet. I know they coming though."

"I used to think it was just old man syndrome, complaining about the way things are in favor of how things used to be. Old men like to let their synapses dry up and complaining is easier than learning to adapt. But we do lose things to the past. You ride the river long enough you see where the rapids are and you get to appreciate the times in between. The older I get, the more I like slowing down. But maybe that's just mortality."

"Tell you what, taking those bullets from you slowed me down plenty. Gave me a lot to think about. In some ways it probably made me stronger. But I needed them, deserved them too, after what I did."

I looked over and he was staring out the passenger window. His reflection in the glass was somber.

"How do you think this ends?" I asked.

"Bad, probably. Things that start bad end bad in my experience. And this started real bad."

I rolled to a stop at an intersection. "Where was it that this started, for you?"

"Day you shot me, or what?"

"Me shooting you was a consequence of you shooting my sister. Had to be down the line from whatever set you on that path. So which choice did that?"

Cassius stared out the windshield at the dimming twilight. I waited.

He finally spoke. "Guess that had to be me taking a dive. There was a dude named Mickey Twitch. Set me up to take a fall in the ring one night. Said he'd take care of things for me after. I'd been working like a dog and not seeing much progress. Mickey's offer sounded like easy money and I was ready for a shortcut. I think I knew at the time I was going down a road that wouldn't end well, but I wanted that pot of gold at the end of the rainbow.

Pretty much had it too, but turned out to all be for nothing. Whole thing went to shit."

"What happened to Mickey Twitch?"

"Don't know. He had me and Johnny on a job that day. Real life pot of gold. Probably still chasing it for all I know. Kinda had that leprechaun look to him, you know?" Cassius cracked a smile. First one I'd seen on him.

A car pulled up behind us at the intersection so I rolled on, but Cassius's comment had my mind working. I tapped the display screen on the Boss. "Hey, Waldo, will you pull up that dash cam footage of the guy we hit with the car?"

Waldo complied with a still image of the scene. I pointed to it. "Any chance that's your leprechaun?"

"Well, damn, that *is* him. You hit him with your car?"

"He showed up the night I found that body in your apartment. Took a shot at me. Then he took more shots after with a rocket launcher. Been trying to figure out how he ties into all this."

Cassius touched the display screen to watch the video. "That's Mickey all right. Looks pissed. Probably 'cause I took all his gold and hid it on him."

I did a double-take. "You did what now?"

Cassius grinned.

I wasn't sure if he was being literal, but whatever he had taken, it would make sense why this Mickey Twitch was so serious about shaking me off the trail. But the Mickey Twitch Cassius knew was in an alternate timeline. If he hid the guy's stash somewhere, it wasn't here, it was there. That would make sense why I ran into him in Cassius's original timeline but *that* Mickey should have nothing to do with this timeline.

Didn't help us here, where Nadia grew up without her brother.

But maybe it connected somehow? Wasn't much more than a hunch but it was something.

"This Mickey guy. Where'd he operate from?"

"Had a boxing bar over on Bellevue. That was the club for the fights, but he did his real work out of a warehouse on this side of town. Maybe half mile that way. Place called Salty Dog Shipping."

"Waldo, can you find that for us?"

Waldo pulled up an address on the screen with a highlighted route.

Only took us a few minutes to get there.

The parking lot was gravel and the Boss's tires made crunching sounds as we rolled up. The sign over the door was rusted and weather-worn but looked like it always had been.

Doors on the warehouse were padlocked. Place looked deserted.

Cassius and I climbed out of the car.

"This the spot?"

"Yeah, this is it."

Night was falling and a low overcast obscured the sky. The headlights from the Boss were all we had to work with out here but it was enough to see by. I retrieved my lock pick set and a flashlight from the car and worked the padlock free from the rolling doors. They groaned when I pushed them open.

As the door yawned wide, the Boss's headlights illuminated a broad vacant space with a catwalk overhead. A second-story office level to the left had windows that overlooked the warehouse floor. Place had been cleared of things that were useful, but there was still trash. Some forklift parts. Some old tires. Shipping pallets were stacked in one corner. My flashlight beam took in the rusting ceiling and dusty windows of the upstairs offices. Then it glinted off something shiny in a seam in the cement floor. I walked over and reached into the seam with my pocket knife. The shiny thing was a bullet casing.

Cassius followed me across the warehouse floor, keeping in range of the flashlight. Looked like someone had used the place to burn donuts. There were tire tracks all over the place.

There was more storage in the back, a walk-in freezer that was no longer cold, a few old brooms and dust pans. Whatever this place had been used for, it was a while ago.

"Salty Dog must be out of business," Cassius said. "This place downright creepy now."

I poked my head into a first-floor room that must have been the lobby. A pedestrian door led outside beyond a standing countertop. A few file cabinets had been left behind and a red phone. There was a false fingernail on the floor partially imbedded in the carpet. It was purple.

I walked back into the main warehouse. A metal staircase led to the second floor. I ascended that and entered the office level. I paused in the hallway because there was damage here. A dent in the sheetrock wall with a dark stain and a door that looked like it had been kicked in. Stain looked like it might be blood.

The office the door led to was vacant, but had two windows that looked out over the warehouse floor and a dried out fish tank that took up most of one wall.

"This used to be Mickey's office," Cassius said.

"Looks like it had new management." I pointed the flashlight beam at a photo on top of a file cabinet that showed a picture of Johnny McKee with his arm around a young Nadia Roseland. They were leaning on the hood of a white Trans Am.

A chair in the middle of the room had tape residue on the arms, but my eyes didn't linger long on that because as my flashlight beam swept the room, my attention was arrested by the stains on the floor. The thin carpet near the desk had been soaked with what appeared to be a large quantity of blood. More on the wall in the corner. Bullet hole in the window. One in the wall. Maybe even one in the ceiling? Furthermore it looked like whoever had been bleeding near the center of the room had at some point been dragged toward the wall near the fish tank. There was a trail.

My stomach churned but I approached anyway, unable to take my eyes off the largest stain. I reached into my pocket as I crouched, and drew a long cylindrical tube from its place inside my jacket. The degravitizer had a test function that made a light glow green if an object was gravitite free but red if the object being tested contained any of the particles making it unstable in time.

I held the degravitizer within an inch of the stain and pressed the test button. The light immediately glowed red.

I stood. "We shouldn't have come in here."

"You think that's blood?"

"And it belongs to a time traveler."

Cassius set his jaw. "Any way we know who that belongs to?"

"Not sure we want to know. But I have a feeling we're going to find out. You were right about one thing. This is all going to end badly."

CHAPTER 38

Mickey Twitch. 1984. Timeline 1.

Mickey Twitch picked up the handset of the payphone on Broad Street. He called the transmitter and entered his account code and waited while the phone clicked and rerouted. He had questions that needed answers and sometimes you had to call somebody.

The phone picked up and a lady's voice said, "Go ahead."

He recognized her voice even though he never knew her name. Knew better than to ask.

"Calling for some information. Need to know about a guy drives a black Mustang that time travels. Tall guy, maybe thirties."

"Hair color?"

"Light brown? I don't know. Kinda sandy? I didn't get a real good look."

"Any other descriptors?"

Mickey rubbed his chin. "His face reminds me of one of them old school guys like maybe you see in a movie."

"Handsome?"

"Yeah, sure, but like a tough guy. Not a pretty boy. A little scruffy."

"Eye color?"

"I don't know, we wasn't staring at each other over soda pop. He was shootin' at me."

"Tag on the car?"

"No. But it was all black, wheels and everything. Late 60s, fastback. Cool as shit, that car. It's a Mustang that travels through time for God's sake. Somebody has to have seen it."

"I'll call you back at this number."

"Yeah, sure. Fine."

He hung up the handset. He'd barely taken his hand off it when it started ringing again. He picked up. "Yeah."

"I have your information. Traveler's name is Greyson Travers, a private detective. Works mostly in the early two-thousands but he's been spotted in other centuries. New York lists him as yellow. Proceed with caution."

"He connected or something?"

"A lot of unknowns on this one. Apparently there is another version of him that's a professor in the twenty-second century but he's listed as off-limits and not an asset. Straight civilian."

"This detective guy plays our side sometimes?"

"Bit of a gray area. He's been rated well as an asset and as an enemy. Choose your poison. Guess he's good to have on your side and rough to go up against, hence the cautionary rating."

"I wreck this guy, does New York care?"

"He's not listed as protected."

"Good, 'cause he's pissing me off."

"Anything else I can assist you with?"

"I don't know. Maybe. This caution rating on this Travers, he got confirmed kills?"

"Yes."

"How many?"

"Several."

"My name's not on that list, is it?"

The pause was longer than he liked, but then she said, "No."

"Okay. That's what I needed to hear. Gonna punch this guy's ticket. You got any leads on where I find him near me?"

"Are you in your local timeline?"

"Me?" That question gave him pause. Would she care that he'd iced the other Mickey in this timeline? "Actually I'm conducting a little business right now. But I can get back to my local. Why? You got a bead on this guy over there?"

"There was a public incident that was registered in a neighboring timeline within a couple of years of your current location. It's the best I can do."

"Gimme that address."

She read it to him.

"Wait, hang on. That's *my* address. That's the warehouse district. You sure that's right?"

"Property owned by Salty Dog Shipping."

"That's *my* company."

"In that year the LLC is managed by a Johnny McKee and a Nadia Roseland."

"What? I just left that place this morning. You telling me in a couple years from now Johnny Fastball is saying *he* runs things?"

"You asked for the information. I don't recommend asking for more if it's going to upset you."

"Then maybe you should get your facts straight!" He slammed the receiver down.

Johnny Fastball running his establishment? Hell no. You throw that guy one frickin' bone and he tries to take over? What nonsense was that? He stared at the phone. Probably shouldn't have hung up on her like that, but too late now. Mickey rolled up his sleeve and started punching keys on his Temprovibe. He got the time coordinates entered and looked around for an anchor.

He still didn't have his gold, but this was all pissing him off. He glared at the street signs. How could he concentrate on getting what was his when people were shanking things from him behind his back? No. He'd deal with Johnny and this Travers guy first. He'd get his hands on that Mustang and come back here to finish up. Once he had that gold, he'd vanish. And wasn't nobody going to be left alive to know better.

He stormed back to the Chrysler and fired it up.

"Please fasten your seatbelt," the car said.

"You say one more thing to me I'll shoot you in the face," Mickey said. But he fastened his seat belt.

"Thank you."

He lurched back into the road and drove.

But he didn't go to the warehouse. Not yet.

He stopped at Gino's place first. He banged on the door. Took two tries before the door opened. Gino's mother had curlers in her hair. He'd seen her around a few times. "Mrs. Russo, how you doin' tonight?"

"Gino's out." She took a look at the Kalashnikov he had slung over his shoulder. "What's that for?"

"Gino's gonna help me shoot some rats."

"Big rats. He's at the bar. The one down the street."

"No matter, he said you wouldn't mind me coming in. Just be a second. I'm sure he'll be home real soon, Mrs. Russo. I'll just wait inside if you don't mind."

"I'm still watching my shows. You like *Trapper John MD*?"

"Never miss an episode, but I'll join you in a few. Just gotta hit the little boys room."

She shuffled toward the kitchen. "Maybe you want a cup of coffee."

Mickey walked left instead and found the nearest bathroom, angling the gun through the doorway. He had his sleeve rolled up and was punching buttons the moment he had the door closed.

The jump didn't change anything in the room from timeline to timeline, except he arrived in the dark. He opened the door and walked out of the bathroom. The TV was still on in this timeline, Mrs. Russo in the living room watching her shows. Mickey slipped out the back door and she never heard him.

He made it back to the sidewalk and of course the Chrysler wasn't there anymore. But he was counting on Gino being a creature of habit. The windfall from this morning might have changed a few things but he doubted it had altered everything. And sure enough, when he located Gino, he was still in the bar buying drinks for anyone in the vicinity. His face lit up when Mickey walked in, then his eyes fell on the gun.

"Bossman! You're walking heavy tonight." He glanced to the back corner.

There were a couple of guys Mickey recognized as cops sitting there, but they were off duty. Neither got up.

"Lighten my load." He unslung the Kalashnikov and passed it to Gino. "You liked that pile I left you this morning?"

"You know it, bossman."

"Time to go earn it."

CHAPTER 39

Greyson. 1988. Timeline 2.

"This is the most relevant information you can find, Waldo?"

Waldo had searched archived local records related to the Salty Dog Shipping property and found several police reports. They showed an incident six months prior where police were called out for a suspected homicide.

Victim's name wasn't available, but there had been a shooting of some kind.

"I can confirm that after the date of the incident, Salty Dog Shipping ceased business and the property was seized by authorities. It's been in a state of flux since, awaiting a government auction. Prior to that it was listed as belonging to Johnny McKee and Nadia Roseland. Whatever happened on that date, it was significant."

"Probably our target date, then. Thanks, Waldo."

"How's this gonna work?" Cassius said. He was in the passenger seat of the Boss watching me mess with the controls.

"We're going to go back in time far enough to intercept this event, whatever it was, and if Heavens is there, I'm going to get her out of there."

"And you're gonna leave my sister be?"

"If you think you can talk sense into her, then fine. Do that. I don't need anyone else to get hurt."

"Only someone does. We know that much. Less somebody was slaughtering time traveling chickens up in that office."

I reached into my pocket. I pulled out the degravitizer and opened the center console of the car. I got as far as sliding out the adapter plug on the end of the unit, but I hesitated.

"What you doing with that?" Cassius asked.

"This device has the ability to test for gravitite particles. When I used it upstairs, it let me know the bloodstains were gravitized, but if I plug it into the car, Waldo can analyze the data and give me a density reading too. Might be enough to give me an idea of whose blood it was."

"But I thought all time travelers have those same particles."

"Not at the same densities. Hold out your arm."

Cassius regarded me with a raised eyebrow but held out an arm. I scanned it with the degravitizer. The light turned red as expected. Then I plugged the device into the car's data port.

"Waldo. What's Cassius's gravitite concentration?"

A graph appeared on the dash screen. Looked about how I expected. I pointed. "This is the minimum viable concentration line. Here is your current value just above that. I'm guessing when you got infused it was some kind of portable device. Maybe some fluid you drank and a homebuilt gravitizer rig?"

Cassius nodded. "Looked like this hokey scaffold but with things all around it to zap you. Felt like I was the project at a kid's science fair."

"Those portable units work but they barely supply enough gravitite particles to get you where you're going. There have been incidents where the concentration density was so low that parts of people got left behind on their first jumps."

"That's disgusting." He looked down at his arm and rubbed it with his other hand. "So if you analyze those readings you took upstairs, you can see if the blood comes from someone like me?"

"Heavens has been a time traveler a long time. Professional infusion, made a lot of jumps since. I was born a time traveler and my mom was too, so I have a higher density than almost anyone I know." I searched for the density results Waldo had taken from me recently and set that on the screen. The comparison between mine and Cassius's numbers was obvious. Mine was hovering near the danger limit.

"Damn," he muttered.

"You've been a time traveler quite a few years but had minimal treatment and only made a few jumps. And now we have a reading from you. I won't know much about your sister's situation, but with process of elimination, we could make some educated guesses."

"Basically you're saying that since you took those readings upstairs, you can find out right now if you or your girl are the ones that get shot or if it's me or my sister."

"That's what I'm saying."

Cassius eyed the center console with more seriousness. "It's like knowing the future, but it being in the past."

"Thing is, once we know it, we know. There's no changing it."

"Like if we know who gets shot, we gotta let that happen?"

"If we don't, we risk creating a paradox, changing the timeline again."

"I think there's been enough of that."

"Me too. But that's what's at stake here."

"That's why you ain't sure you want to know."

I looked back to the warehouse and its rusted sign. The old

dog on it was so faded it was getting hard to make out. "I don't think anything can change the course of what's going to happen here. It feels like it's been coming for a while. Not looking forward to anyone else getting hurt. But whatever goes down, I want it to end here." I rested a hand on the steering wheel. "But for what it's worth, I think I'm done hating you."

"Why?"

"I don't know."

"I guess it's still something. Don't think I hate you much anymore either. So long as you don't screw that up tonight." He looked down at the gravitizer unit. "May as well do it then. If we both agreed what happens happens, then I guess knowing won't change it. But I think I want to know. Could be some time travelers we never met, right?"

"Maybe. Unlikely though."

Cassius crossed his arms and waited.

I sighed, and spoke. "Waldo, I'd like a gravitite density check on the readings I took upstairs."

"I'll put the results on the screen."

The analysis didn't take long. They began popping up in the reverse order of how I took them.

The first didn't match anything I'd seen so far. Nor the second.

But when the third density graph appeared, there was no mistaking it. It was identical to one of the other graphs already on the screen.

The blood was mine.

CHAPTER 40

Greyson. 1988. Timeline 2.

Time is a relative thing. There was a way I could dodge this. Could be this was my end, but it didn't have to be right now. I could still vamoose and go sit on a beach somewhere with a cold drink and a tropical view. Might be able to drag that out for years.

But I wasn't much for procrastination. And impending doom tends to spoil the flavor of even the best margarita.

This was happening now. Or six months ago if I put it in linear time.. I'd waited long enough.

Waldo had done some scans and flashed a tiny camera back in time to our destination date. It was usually used to find alternative parking spaces and dodge meter maids but it came in handy for this situation too.

We only had a view inside the warehouse for a half-second window but it told us a lot. Good place to land, for one. Also some of what we were up against.

The place had guards and the fish-eye view from the camera was even good enough for Cassius to identify Johnny Fastball on a catwalk. Plenty of guns in view.

I got out to open the trunk of the Boss, and pulled up the floor. It wasn't much of an arsenal, but I stored a shotgun and a spare pistol there. This one wasn't coded to my palm or the chip in my ring so I handed it to Cassius.

"Guess I'm breaking my parole some more today," he said as he took the gun. He wasn't supposed to be time traveling either but it was that kind of day.

"If you end up in trouble, say I kidnapped you and this was your only option. Convincing people I wanted to kill you won't be a hard sell."

He held the gun in his palm and felt the weight of it.

"Ain't touched one of these since the day it all went down. Never thought I would again."

"I'm not saying we have to kill anybody in there, but this isn't a setup wildly suited for calm conversation."

"You got a plan beyond going in guns blazing? From what I can tell, there's lots of them and only two of us."

"Three," I said. "We've got Waldo. You'd be surprised how useful he can be in a fight." I loaded some less-lethal rubber pellet shotgun shells into the shotgun and my pockets and closed the trunk of the Boss.

"So, guns and car blazing?"

I checked the load in my Stinger 1911. These were all standard rounds. Plenty lethal. "We get in, get Heavens out, that's all we need to do."

"Only you got this look in your eye says you going to tear shit up. If you're on a kamikaze mission, I don't feel great about being included."

"Just stick close. Be ready to talk some sense into your sister. From what I can tell, you're the only one nobody has any reason to want to kill."

"That's only because everyone already thinks I'm dead."

"Handy, right?"

I walked toward the warehouse carrying the shotgun and slipped on my shades.

"We ain't driving in?"

"We'll use my chronometer while Waldo has some fun."

Waldo spoke in my earpiece. "You think taking fire as a diversion counts as fun?"

"I'm counting on you to drive fast enough that they'll miss."

"And how does that help you?"

"Don't worry about me, buddy. Whatever happens to me is what I've had coming for a while."

"Somehow that doesn't make me feel better."

"Maybe you can get that easier job you always wanted. Air traffic control, was it?"

"My record of failing to avoid calamity may not look good on my resumé."

"This is just another day on the job, Waldo. All had to end sometime."

Waldo's half-second scan of the past had given me enough of a view to spot a decent jump location inside the warehouse. It was close to the stairs heading up to the offices. The place was dusty and dead quiet. I took a breath in the silence. Things would get loud quick in here.

I synced the time on my chronometer to Waldo's estimated jump coordinates and found a spot just out of view of his camera.

Cassius caught up. Waldo drove the Boss through the warehouse doors and idled in the open, the gas engine running. He revved it once and waited.

Cassius had both hands on the pistol I'd given him, but he trembled a little.

"Don't worry. This is all going to go down fast. Over before you know it."

"Maybe that's what I'm worried about."

205

I cradled the shotgun and placed my chronometer hand to an exposed girder. "Hang on to me."

Cassius rested one hand on my shoulder.

Waldo revved the engine again and kept the RPM high this time. The car pulsed with the barely contained power.

The timer on the chronometer ticked down. Then we jumped.

We showed up a fraction of a second ahead of Waldo and the Boss.

Hard to describe the sound of a car ripping through time into a closed warehouse mid-burnout, but it was loud. Rubber shrieked on the concrete and the roar of the engine echoed off the walls. Turning heads was something the Boss was always good at. And it was what I was counting on.

The moment we arrived in the past, I was moving, Cassius rushing to keep up.

It was only seconds till the gunfire erupted, but by then I was already headed up the stairs, riot shotgun at the ready. Noise from the warehouse floor obscured our footfalls on the stairs enough that when the guy at the top came into view he was completely caught off guard. His gun came up but nowhere near fast enough. I pulled the trigger and the rubber round caught him in the upper chest sending him spinning backward. The pistol flew out of his hand and went skidding down the hall. The guy himself collided with the wall and managed to stay on his feet long enough to get the butt end of my shotgun across his jaw. Then he went down hard.

I stepped over him and ran fast for the door we'd already identified as Mickey Twitch's office. Another guard appeared at the end of the hall and I fired. This time the rubber round put the guy into the wall behind him so hard he didn't even wiggle when he collapsed. He might be getting back up, but no time soon.

Big things were crashing into each other down in the

warehouse. Sounded like Waldo was bowling through shipping crates with the Boss. There was enough gunfire for a small army, but I doubted it had been enough to obscure the sound of the shotgun.

Whatever was on the other side of Mickey Twitch's office door had to know I was coming.

But Cassius squared up next to me anyway.

"You ready for this?" I asked.

"Hell no. But let's do it."

We rushed the door.

CHAPTER 41

Nadia. 1988. Timeline 2.

Nadia knew he'd come. But the car was a surprise.

The warehouse looked like a lightning storm with muzzle flashes coming from every direction. The Mustang had made a full circuit of the warehouse with bullets spraying off the concrete in its wake. Now it kept disappearing and reappearing around the warehouse and causing havoc. How was it doing that? Those windows were too dark to see through but Nadia knew better than to worry.

Greyson Travers wasn't going to die in a barrage of gunfire in his car.

She was going to kill him herself.

Heavens Archer sat tense in the chair, ducking slightly. Hard to help it with so many bullets flying around the place. Nadia felt like cowering too, but she didn't. She set her Temprovibe instead.

It was simple enough. She knew this room. She had her moment in the past selected. When Greyson Travers burst in or appeared via time travel, she'd vanish the same instant. But she'd come back to put a bullet in him before he could move. She'd practiced.

This wasn't going to be a fight. It was chess. And she was great at chess.

The report from the shotgun in the hall turned her head. Heavens looked too.

Nadia had the Temprovibe on her right arm and her gun in that hand as well. She pointed it toward the door just in case. Her left hand was poised over the jump button. Feet planted. When she pressed the button, she'd come back to this same location but walk eight feet closer once she knew where his head would be. She'd walk it calmly, just like she'd practiced. All the time in the world on the night she'd saved for this. Just the empty office from a few weeks ago. Walk that eight feet. Raise the gun. Jump back, fire.

Greyson Travers would die fast.

She regretted that she couldn't find some way to torture him a little, but that would've been too risky. Too much time. She couldn't let him have that. Time travelers could do a lot with a few seconds. Another reason she'd have to kill Heavens afterward. That was a pity. She really did like the woman. She'd held up far better to being kidnapped than she'd expected. But there was no letting her go now. What was done was done. Nadia had made peace with the fact that there would be collateral damage with her revenge. Greyson should've thought of that before he killed her brother. Heavens' death would be on him. But Johnny had promised he'd be the one to get rid of Heavens. She appreciated that. Knowing it had to happen was one thing. Doing it would be another.

But Greyson she would kill herself.

This was almost over.

The door burst open like a train had hit it. Her finger hovered over the jump button. All senses trained on that doorway. See his position and go.

And there he was.

She pressed the button.

And she blinked.

Then she gasped.

What the hell? She stared at the empty office, serenely lit, the door still closed here.

She hadn't seen it right. In that doorway.

It had looked like . . .

Was it her mind playing tricks on her?

She stood there. She was supposed to be walking. Eight feet, raise the gun, jump back. Squeeze the trigger.

But the other man in that doorway.

Cass?

Her body shook. The gun in her hand shook. This was adrenaline, that's all. Cassius was dead. She *saw* his body. She'd only seen someone who looked like him. Of course he'd been on her mind. This was *all* about Cassius. Was it so strange that her mind would play tricks on her under a moment of stress?

She took one step, then another. Cassius was dead. If he'd been alive, he'd have contacted her. It was another man. Someone who looked like him. Some friend Travers had brought along. This guy was older, wasn't he? Not Cass's age. Probably forty. Too old to be him.

She'd stopped walking.

"Get it together," she muttered. "Now." She kept going. Five more steps. She made it to the door. Turned. She lifted the gun to where she'd seen Greyson Travers. Right about here, wasn't it?

But that other man was right next to him. If she shot Greyson from this angle would it kill that guy too? It might. Close range. She didn't know.

What if she missed and hit Cass?

No. It wasn't Cass. That was impossible.

She blew out a long breath. Reached for her Temprovibe and reset it. She'd practiced this. This was supposed to be easy. Push the button, squeeze the trigger.

Push the button, squeeze the trigger.

Push . . The . . . Button.

How many years had she prepared for this? All that time. All the sacrifices she'd made to set things right. This was going to restore balance. Greyson Travers shouldn't be allowed to walk the earth if her brother couldn't.

Her brother.

What if it was really him?

God she missed him.

Her eyes watered. What was happening? She wasn't supposed to be crying. She was so close.

"I've come too far," she said to the empty room. "There's no going back now." It was the same thing she'd told herself when she took Heavens. But her resolve didn't harden this time when she said it. She was about to jump back and end this.

"Damn it, Cass. What am I supposed to do?"

She shivered. Why was this so hard?

She was the one with the gun. She had the Temprovibe. She was in control here.

"Greyson Travers deserves to die."

And that was still true. Her mind didn't reject anything about that statement.

That was enough. She held on to the thought. Her truth. Her compass.

"Greyson Travers is *going* to die," she said to the room. She raised the gun again. Jaw clenched, she put her free hand to the Temprovibe. Finger poised. Other index finger on the trigger of her gun. Ready. She pressed the button.

CHAPTER 42

Greyson. 1988. Timeline 2.

A lot can happen in a split-second.

Cassius and I went through the door together, bursting in with the force of a tornado. I was still holding the shotgun, which in hindsight would occur to me as a mistake. Made it too hard to get to my chronometer. But I didn't get much time for hindsight.

The first half-second view we had of the room showed Heavens in a chair, bound and wide-eyed, her mouth forming a shout of warning. Nadia Roseland was there too, pistol aimed in our direction.

But then she was gone. Vanished like a misplaced thought.

And I knew I was in trouble.

I'd been ready for guns. As ready as you can be anyway.

Staring down the barrel of a gun and squeezing a trigger is harder than they make it look in the movies. Taking a life isn't easy. People miss a lot with guns and if that's what she had stuck with, I would have been okay with it. The odds were in my favor.

But people don't miss with time travel.

Time travel gives you time to think. To plan. To be sure. Time travelers have all the advantages.

And by the time I'd released my grip on the shotgun and reached for my own chronometer, it was too late.

My weapon hadn't even hit the floor when she reappeared. The barrel of her pistol was aimed at my face. A range you don't miss at.

And in that instant I was a dead man.

If she had stayed in that instant with me, all that hate in her eyes, it would have been my last. But her eyes didn't stay on me. They drifted. Pulled by a force stronger than gravity. They shifted past me. To Cassius.

A lot can happen in the rest of a split-second. Recognition. Shock. Hesitation. Another split-second to live.

I ducked.

And maybe it was the movement that jarred her. The reaction. Squeezing that trigger.

The gun rocked in her hand, bullet exploding from the barrel in a deafening bang. The place my head had just been.

And in the next half-second, I was still there. Head still attached and able to turn.

Cassius hadn't ducked.

But shooting people is hard.

People miss a lot with guns.

Nadia Roseland had missed.

And when I stood back up, hand on my chronometer, ready to jump away, she was still staring at Cassius. He stared back.

"Hey, little sis."

She still had the gun. Finger still on the trigger. But Cassius seemed to ignore it. His own gun was low at his side.

Nadia's mouth was open but it took a moment to make any sound. "I almost killed you."

Cassius glanced down and checked himself briefly. "I'm still here."

She finally lowered the gun.

"How?" She gaped, taking him in.

"Kind of a long story. Fourteen years long for me. Looks like it's been a few for you, too." He glanced at me. Nadia did too. But her eyes didn't burn like they did before. The hate was diffused by something else. She looked back to Cassius, too curious to keep her eyes from him.

Heavens was my only focus. I wasn't actively being shot at so I crossed quickly to where she was bound and stooped behind her, retrieving my pocket knife and setting to work on her bonds.

Nadia saw me but her objections died in her mouth when Cassius stepped forward and wrapped her in his arms. Her gun hand fell to her side and she turned into him, succumbing to the moment.

"About time you got here," Heavens whispered.

I put a hand on her shoulder and leaned in close. "I've got you. Almost out of this."

The gunfire in the warehouse had ceased.

Wasn't sure what that meant, but a quiet had descended on the building.

Whole place smelled like gun smoke.

I got Heavens up from her chair. Getting her out of there fast was my only plan. I reached for my pistol but she put a hand on my arm and spoke. "Nadia."

Nadia was in a state of shock from the look of her, but she turned her attention to Heavens.

"You're going to be okay," Heavens said. "This wasn't your fault."

She was doing that thing again. Something I'd watched her do before. Seeing past the situation to the people in it. Seeing something in Nadia that needed addressing. Something beyond her own anger at being kidnapped. I didn't feel it. I was still angry. But I could see she needed to say it. So I waited.

"I have so many questions," Nadia said.

"And we'll help you," Heavens said. "I have plenty of questions myself. But this needs to end."

Nadia looked down at the gun still in her hand. Cassius put his hand out for it. "I can help."

And Nadia did it. She slowly handed the gun to Cassius and let out a breath. One she looked like she'd been holding for a long time.

And in that split-second, everything seemed like it was going to work out okay.

But a lot can happen in the other half of a split-second.

I caught their reflection in the fish tank first.

Two of them. Both with guns, appearing behind me and Heavens.

I turned in time to see him lift his pistol.

Mickey Twitch and some guy I didn't know holding a rifle that looked military issue. Mickey was aiming his revolver at the only other guy in the room still holding guns. Cassius Roseland.

"Having a party in my office without me?" Mickey asked.

Nadia shrieked.

She moved behind Cassius. And he tried to raise his hands. But he was still holding those guns. He wasn't trying to shoot. He was trying to put his hands up, but in that split-second I knew Mickey didn't see it that way. And he had his finger on the trigger.

I've done a lot of stupid things in my day. And drawing down on two guys at once counts on that list. But doing so while stepping into the line of fire really takes the cake.

I shot from the hip and got one good shot off. It hit the big guy with the semiautomatic rifle and sent him reeling. But when I tried to strafe left and get Mickey too, I was too slow.

My shot went wide and his muzzle flashed. I took the hit in my chest.

I fell to the ground and found myself staring up at the florescent lights of the ceiling. Heavens screamed.

Don't know what happened in the next half-second. Pretty sure my eyes were closed.

But when I opened them again Mickey was still holding a smoking gun. Nobody else had been stupid enough to get shot. Cassius had dropped his guns and put both hands up.

"Anybody else want to be a fucking hero?" Mickey screamed.

I groaned. I leaned my head back to stare at the ceiling some more.

At least now I knew where all my blood had come from.

CHAPTER 43

Mickey Twitch. 1988. Timeline 2.

What Mickey Twitch hated more than anything, was losing control of a situation. This one had almost gotten out of hand.

If he hadn't had the drop on this bunch, it might have gone different. Even so, Gino was on the ground moaning and doing him no good.

You go time traveling for one day and everything goes to hell.

Mickey stooped and picked up the Kalashnikov from where Gino had dropped it. He aimed it at the remaining members of the group and tucked his pistol back into the waistband of his pants.

Did they really think they could pull one over on him in *his* office?

At least it looked like they'd done a good job keeping his fish alive in the intervening years.

"Okay. Now which one of you shitbags is going to tell me what's going on around here?"

But before anyone could respond, there were footfalls on the stairs. Someone coming up. Johnny Fastball appeared in the ruined doorway, out of breath, holding a pistol.

"Heard the shots, babe, did you get him—" His words faded on his lips when he caught sight of the group. "Cassius? Mickey?" He took in the bleeding guy on the floor too. Travers. The stunner blonde had worked her way over to him and was cradling his head in her lap. Looked like he might still be alive.

"How you doing, Johnny?" Mickey said. "I hear you think you run things now."

Johnny gawped at him. "You . . . You were gone, Mick. So we did what we could with things. Didn't know if you were coming back." He looked to the girl, questioning.

Nadia. Guess she was the real boss here. The balls on this one.

"How about you try running this, Johnny?" Mickey squeezed the trigger on the Kalashnikov and put three rounds into Johnny. He stumbled back into the hall and went down. Nadia screamed.

Glad he had her attention now.

Huh. Guess this gun wasn't so bad after all.

The blonde was eyeing her boyfriend's pistol lying on the floor a few feet from him.

"Oh you think you want this?" Mickey took a step forward and hooked the gun with his shoe, kicking it away till it hit the base of the fish tank behind him.

"Anyone else have any great ideas?"

No one spoke.

So he aimed the rifle at Cassius next.

"You have something that belongs to me."

Cassius had dropped the guns he'd been holding. He kicked them away voluntarily. "Don't need no trouble, Mickey. I came for Nadia and that's it. You let her go, I'll tell you right where it is."

"Noble. Tell me now. Then we see about what to do with your sister."

"You know I can't do that, Mickey. Not till she's safe."

"What about her? You want *her* safe?" He aimed the gun at the blonde. She was clutching at her bleeding boyfriend's hand.

"Don't hurt them either."

"Where's my gold, Cassius?"

Cassius opened his mouth to speak but closed it again, then he smiled.

"You think something's funny?" Mickey said. "How about this for funny?" He turned back to the blonde, ready to splatter her brains across the floor, but she wasn't there. Travers either. Shit. She hadn't been holding his hand. It was that *watch*. He spun in place, searching, but they were nowhere to be found. "Shit!" he shouted. "Shit!" Then he turned back to Cassius. He was ready to end all of this right now. But he'd shoot the sister first.

"Hey, Mickey." The voice came from near the fish tank this time. He turned and found the nearly unconscious Travers propped up against the blonde again, this time with his gun in his hand. She was helping him aim it and had her finger on the trigger.

"We're back," Travers said. And the blonde squeezed the trigger.

The last thing that went through Mickey Twitch's head was a bullet.

CHAPTER 44

Greyson. 1988. Timeline 2.

I woke in a hospital bed with what looked like morning sun coming through the window.

Took a few blinks to figure out I wasn't alone. There was a woman in the chair next to me.

"Heavens?" I murmured.

But when the woman rose and stood over me, it wasn't Heavens. Her freckled nose and sincere brown eyes were a welcome sight though.

"Hey, little brother. Good to have you back."

Piper looked like she'd been awake all night, but still had all her class, wearing a silk blouse and at least some of her best jewelry. She smiled at me. "Sent Heavens home to get some rest. Expect she'll be back shortly. She's been here for most of the last thirty-six hours. Had to pry her away."

"I got shot."

"I noticed."

There were a lot of monitors in the room but none were

beeping excessively. If I was dying, I imagined they'd have more to say. I tried sitting up but everything hurt so I quit.

"You're going to be down for a bit. But you're expected to recover. Did you know the vast majority of penetrative chest wounds aren't fatal? Assuming they aren't cardiac."

"You've been doing your research."

"Didn't want you to get a big head thinking you were special. Even the guy you allegedly shot in the chest is supposed to survive."

"Machine gun guy?"

"Someone named Eugenio Russo? Known underworld meathead. Heard he has the IQ of a rock. If that guy can survive a chest wound, I knew you had to. Otherwise I'd never let you live it down."

I felt the bandages on my chest. "Feel like I got punched in the lungs."

"Pressure on your chest. But you have a chest tube for drainage. You're lucky. Doctor said you dodged a few really bad ways to go. Bullet came out your back and you lost a lot of blood. But you avoided major surgery. Want to ask me what a thoracotomy is?"

"Did I have one of those?"

"No, thankfully. Partly why you're in recovery. But I looked it up. I can tell you all about them. Sternotomies and anterolateral incisions too. Ask me about any of it."

"Now you're just showing off."

"Had a lot of reading time." Piper pulled her chair around to have a better view of me and sat. "So. Heavens said the bullet you stepped in front of was meant for Cassius Roseland."

"Talk about dumb moves, huh?"

She reached for my hand. "I'm proud of you."

I squeezed her fingers. "Turns out he's not the same guy as he was when I first met him."

"Is this you admitting people can change?"

"Hated him for a long time. Took a while to get around to seeing how much it was weighing me down, but it was."

"I appreciate whatever you did to make sure I'm still here. But I'm glad you found a way to forgive him. Maybe forgive yourself in the process?"

"Maybe. I thought he deserved every bit of it, but what I did didn't make things right. I have to admit, I don't know where this leaves me."

She pressed my hand between both of hers. "Free of it?"

I could admit that sounded pretty good.

Piper and I talked for the next hour, till Heavens arrived. Her reassuring smile when she walked in was more soothing than any of the drugs they had me on, but she wasn't alone. Agent Jonathan Black Elk was with her. He was back in uniform and looked larger than life again. His face was grave. He closed the door behind him.

Heavens made straight for the side of my bed and took a seat on the edge next to me, ignoring the others in the room and leaning directly over to press her lips to mine.

I was so caught off guard it took a moment for my brain to catch up. By then she had pulled her face away.

Holy hell.

"That's for coming to my rescue," she whispered. She then took my face in both of her hands and kissed me again, this time firmer, her lips parting mine and her warm breath in my mouth. When she pulled away the second time she said, "That one is because I've wanted to."

"Okay then," I said, too surprised to form a coherent thought beyond that.

Jonathan Black Elk cleared his throat.

"Not to interrupt, but when I heard you were awake, I wanted to come get your statement. Have a few things to clarify about how you came in. And the office wanted me to talk to you straight away, before things could get . . . muddled."

I groaned as I shifted on the bed. "Do I need a lawyer present?"

"Not as of yet. But it's your call."

I sized him up. "I trust you. What do you want to know?"

Piper stood and offered Black Elk her chair. "I was just heading out anyway." She leaned over and met my eye. "You call me if you need me, okay?"

"Thank you for being here."

She squeezed my hand. "It's what we do, right?"

Heavens reached for her hand as she passed as well, and the two women shared brief reassuring smiles.

When Piper was gone, Black Elk settled into the chair and pulled out a tablet to record with. Heavens stayed, but he made no objection.

Black Elk eyed the monitors. "Seems your penchant for finding trouble hasn't lessened over the years," he said. "What can you tell me about the demise of Mickey Twitch?"

"*I* shot Mickey Twitch," Heavens said. "You should probably ask me that question."

Black Elk raised an eyebrow. "With Greyson's gun?"

Heavens lifted my right hand and wrapped both of hers around it, miming how she had used the gun. "Greyson was nearly unconscious at the time."

"I get the assist though, right?" I said.

She set my hand down. "Mickey Twitch had just killed one his former associates and was about to murder Cassius and Nadia Roseland. Shooting him was our only option to save them. And he'd already shot Greyson."

"Okay." Black Elk looked to me. "That how you saw it too?"

"It was memorable. And it's the truth of what happened."

"And how did Cassius Roseland, a parolee from a different timeline, happen to be there?"

"I strongly persuaded him," I said. "While searching for Heavens."

"How strong of a persuasion are we talking?"

"You can phrase it any way you want to the parole board, but he was only doing it to protect his sister. Not his fault for being there. It was mine."

"You have any thoughts as to the current whereabouts of Mr. Roseland and his sister? I'd like to chat with them too."

"Not sure I even know my own whereabouts at the moment. But they don't appear to be in this room."

Black Elk pressed stop on his tablet recorder and rested it on the bed. Then he folded his hands in his lap. "I'm sure there will be more follow-up questions, but as far as I'm concerned, I've checked the boxes I need to for the moment. Mickey Twitch was a low level cog in the larger machine connected to New York and the Amadeus organization. His underlings that met their demise barely registered on the map when it comes to individuals we have an interest in. But I think the general concern of the agency is as to whether we can expect any more violence related to this incident."

I exhaled slowly. It only hurt a little. "Book's closed as far as I'm concerned."

He turned to Heavens. "And am I to understand you still don't intend to press charges against Nadia Roseland for abducting you?"

This was news to me, so I was just as interested in the response.

"Since it's my choice, that's what I've decided. I don't think there is anything to be gained for anyone from locking that young woman up."

"The agency would like me to strongly recommend you reconsider."

"And you can tell the agency I recommend they stick it in their ear."

Black Elk cracked a smile. "You'd be surprised how often I hear that. Though it's not always that particular bit of anatomy."

He sighed, then rose. "I've only got a month on my clock till retirement. I'd say I hope to see you both again, but I don't. Not in an official capacity anyway. But I'm going to file my reports and cross my fingers that you two can stay out of trouble at least *that* long."

"Model citizenship going on over here," I said, with a vague wave to encompass my bed situation. "How much trouble can I get into while horizontal?"

Black Elk walked to the door and gave us one last nod. "Try not to wander too far if we need you. Someone will be in touch."

I waved as he walked out and shut the door. Then I turned to Heavens. "That was a lie, by the way. I can get into all kinds of trouble while horizontal."

She laughed so fast she snorted a little, and that made me laugh too. It hurt like hell but I didn't regret it.

When she calmed down and my ribs stopped hurting, she leaned over me again. I liked the view.

She was looking at me in a way that was definitely more than just friends.

"Can I ask what happened to change your mind on us?" I asked. "Or was this what your future self told you would happen?"

Heavens put a hand to my face. "Only thing she said was that I'd know when you were ready because you'd finally let go of your past. I had no idea what that meant. But watching you step in front of a gun for Cassius and Nadia made it pretty clear you've done that."

"You mean all I had to do to get you to kiss me was take a bullet for somebody? Should have told me that day one."

"I could still be wrong. Maybe I've screwed up the future now and created a paradox from which our timelines will never recover."

I lifted my hand and put my fingers to the back of her head. "Let's make sure we screw it up right then."

She smiled and let me pull her lips to mine.

And paradox or not, that kiss was worth it.

CHAPTER 45

Greyson. 1988. Timeline 2.

Heavens sprung me from the hospital as soon as I was able to get out of bed. I had to be wheeled out, but my own pains were quickly forgotten when I saw the Boss pull up to the curb.

"Oh. Waldo. What did you do?"

The car had dozens of bullet holes in it and the rear window was gone. The windshield had holes in it too. I cringed at the spare tire and the gouges in the fenders, but it was still rolling. Heavens helped me into the passenger seat, which also had bullet holes in it.

"I thought you were going to drive faster, buddy."

Waldo's voice came from only one functional speaker. "If you counted the amount of shots fired, my rate of avoidance would seem more impressive. But you did ask for a diversion."

"You did good, man. I guess the Boss and I can recuperate together."

Heavens climbed into the driver's seat and programmed the jump controls. Mercifully the time traveling operations of the car had been preserved.

I tried to ignore all the obvious damage around us. "Heavens, next time you get kidnapped, I'm going to borrow *your* car."

Heavens laughed and patted the dashboard. "But then Waldo wouldn't get to be my valiant hero."

"Waldo's the hero?"

"Everyone knows that," she said as she shifted into gear. "Let's get you boys home."

Recovering at the Rose 'n Bridge had its perks. I wasn't supposed to be drinking caffeine or alcohol for a while but what my doctors didn't know wouldn't kill them. I did take it easy though and took my coffee with a little bit of milk for a change.

The inn was now touring the 1990s, so the guests were really into flannel and Nirvana at the moment. I had shuffled my way downstairs to my usual spot at the bar and was enjoying my coffee to the sounds of *Smells Like Teen Spirit* when I had a visitor.

Cassius Roseland walked in. It was the mirror image of the day I'd come in and shot him in this same room, and for just a moment I had the urge to reach for a gun. But he closed the distance quickly and put a hand out. I took hold of it. Fourteen years full circle.

"Heard you were here. Wanted to make sure you were okay," he said.

"I should be," I said. "If I can learn to keep better company."

He grinned. "Better low class than no class."

"How's Nadia?"

"She's all right. Keeping a low profile for a bit. Things are still confusing at the moment. But we're getting it figured out."

I gestured to the stool next to me. "You have time for a drink?"

"I can make time."

"Did still have one question rattling around my head for you."

"Shoot," he said. But then threw up his hands. "Not really though." He grinned.

"You're hilarious."

"'Bout all we can do is laugh about it now, right?"

"Beats the alternative." I sipped my coffee. "So, the other night Mickey Twitch was screaming at you about his money. Said you knew where all his gold was. You ever go get it?"

Cassius gave a wan smile. "That your way of asking where it is? How dumb you think I'd have to be to tell something like that to a time traveler?"

I tried to look shocked. "You don't think you can trust *me*?"

He looked me in the eye and held it. "Yeah, I actually think I might, now. But it don't matter anyway. Gold's not there anymore. I checked."

"Ah. At least you don't seem upset about it."

He smiled again. "An old blind guy owned the place I stashed it. He don't live there anymore though. You should see his new house. Place has three tennis courts. I ask you what a blind man needs with three tennis courts."

I laughed. "Less blind than you thought?"

"I guess. Maybe he can still make out those little tennis skirts girls wear. Beats me. But I guess when you suddenly rich you do what you want."

"You ever think maybe you went back in time and got the gold and just gave him enough for that place with the tennis courts?"

Cassius stared. "You kidding me?"

I shrugged. "No paradox there, is it? It's what I would do if I were you."

He tapped his temple with a forefinger. "That's why people can tell you're a born time traveler. You think like one."

229

Heavens walked over and greeted him. She had a rum and Coke in her hand. "Good to have you back under better circumstances," she said. It was easy to sense the relief he felt at being here safely. He was taking in the place with a sense of wonder.

Eventually he turned back to me. "I ever do get my hands on that money, I think I'm coming back for one of these vacations."

"You don't need a pile of gold for that," I said. "You've got friends in the business now." I gestured to Heavens.

She put a hand out and rested it on his atop the bar. "And you can bring Nadia. Tell her I said so."

Cassius clenched her hand then went for his drink. His hand was shaking a little as he lifted it and his eyes were watery, but I did my best not to notice.

We had our drinks in peace instead.

It was only fifteen minutes or so later when Violet, the alternate bartender, walked up behind us. "Hey, Mr. Travers?"

I swiveled on my stool. "You know you can call me Greyson by now, right?"

"Sorry, yeah. It's just what I'm used to calling you. But there's a man over in the restaurant section, says he's looking for the private detective. I think he means you?"

"He give a name?"

"No. But he looks kind of familiar for some reason. I don't think he's been in before but he was asking for you. Said I should be discreet?" She gave a shrug.

"Sure. Point him out to me, will you?" I slid gingerly off my stool and walked slowly around the corner of the divider that blocked some of the pub from the usually rowdier bar section. Violet let me lean on her a little as we went.

"That's him, over there in the booth. The one in the tweed jacket."

The man was only in his forties but wore glasses and had a

smattering of gray at his temples. He had a sincere face and was surreptitiously surveying the tavern with interest from behind his menu. He also had a brown leather journal he kept scribbling notes in with a pencil.

"Holy shit," I muttered.

"You know him?" Violet said.

"I've never seen him this *young* before."

"Who is he?"

"That's Dr. Harold Quickly."

"The inventor? Didn't he like, invent all of this?" She gestured vaguely to the tavern.

I knew what she meant. I checked the current date on my chronometer. Mid-nineties. Good gracious.

"That man's . . . my grandfather," I said. "And I think this could be his first time time traveling."

Violet's eyes widened. "Does he know you're his grandson?"

The man at the table kept scribbling notes.

"I'm not sure he even knows where he is."

"Whoa," Violet muttered. "What are you going to do?"

I slipped my chronometer off my wrist and put it in my pocket. "I think I'm going to go see what he wants."

THE END.

Thanks for reading! Greyson's adventures will continue.

Check for the latest *Paradox PI* mysteries at:

mybook.to/Paradox-PI-Series

If you would like to dive into another time travel adventure right now, you can read the series that started it all featuring Greyson's father, Ben Travers, and the mysterious Doctor Quickly.

IN TIMES LIKE THESE

"Don't assume that because you know something in the future won't happen, that you can do nothing. Sometimes the reason it doesn't happen is you."
  -Excerpt from the journal of Dr. Harold Quickly, 1997

Chapter 1

I have far too much of my life in my arms to even think of reaching for my phone when it starts ringing in my pocket. I concentrate on getting the key in the lock. That and not dropping the shoes, water bottles and mail I've hauled to the door of my apartment. I get the door open with my free fingers and just make it inside when one of the water bottles escapes. The next moment, all but my useless junk mail is on the living room floor. I leave it there and open my phone the moment before it gives up on me.

"Hey, Carson. What's up?"

"Dude. You coming to batting practice?"

"I'll be there. Just got home from work."

"Okay, can you check the weather while you're there?"

"No problem. See you in a few."

I toss my phone and the junk mail onto the couch and locate the remote in the cushions. The station is still on commercials, so I head for the kitchen. Depositing the remote on the counter, I turn to the refrigerator out of habit. It's still just as sparse as the last time I checked. I settle for my one remaining bottle of water and head for the bedroom to change. The news broadcast comes on from around the corner.

"Welcome back to News Channel 8. In a few moments we'll get your Drive Time Traffic and weather, but first, a look at today's top stories.

"Today was the conclusion of the eight month trial of Elton Stenger, the man accused of murdering fourteen people in a series of vicious car bombings and shootings throughout the state of Florida. Judge Alan Waters ruled today that Stenger be convicted, and serve fourteen consecutive life sentences, a record number for the state of Florida. Stenger is being transported today into federal custody and will be tried in the state of New York for three additional murders."

I pull my paycheck from my shorts pocket and lay it on the dresser. It'll be gone in a week. Emptying the meager contents of my wallet out next to the check, I extract enough cash for a couple of post-game beers. *Minimal celebrating is still better than no celebrating.*

"Today is a monumental day for St. Petersburg and the entire scientific community, as the St. Petersburg Temporal Studies Society gets set to test their latest particle accelerator, what they claim may be the world's first time machine. They will attempt to launch a number of particles through time and space in their laboratory here in St. Petersburg today.

"We have correspondent David Powers on the scene. David, what's going on down there?"

I get into my athletic shorts and snag some socks. *Where the hell did I put my uniform shirt?* I cruise through the living room to head for my laundry closet.

" . . . and while the potential applications of the experiment are yet to be determined, one thing is for certain, these researchers won't be wasting any time. Back to you, Barbara."

I glimpse the blonde woman grinning on screen with her co-anchor. "Next thing we know they'll be rolling out a Delorean. Certainly a day to remember. Now we go to Carl Sims with our weather update."

I know what it's going to say. Hot. Chance of thunderstorms. This is Florida. I locate my wrinkled *Hit Storm* shirt in the laundry basket, and slide it over my head as I walk back around the corner to the TV. Just as expected, the little cloud and lightning symbol dominates the entire week.

When I arrive at the field, most of the team is already there. I spot Carson's orange hair as he's out on the mound throwing batting practice. As I step out of my car, the moist, sweet smell of clay and grass clippings makes my shoulders relax. Each step I take toward the field helps the tension of my workday ebb away. Robbie is donning his cleats in the dugout as I walk up.

"Hey, man." I throw my glove into the cubby beside his.

"What's up, Ben? How's it going?"

"Hoping we're going to get to play this one," I reply.

"Yeah me too, I'm going to forget how to swing a bat if we keep getting rained out." Robbie stands and stretches his arms toward the roof of the dugout. My arms would reach it. At 5'8" Robbie's come up short. What he lacks in height he makes up for in fitness. Despite his on again, off again cigarette habit, he can still out-sprint anyone on the team. His lean and muscular physique is contrasted by his relaxed demeanor; a constant state of ease that makes me feel like I'm rushing through life by comparison.

"Have we got enough people tonight? I know Nick said he was going to be out of town in Georgia or something like that." I kick off my flip-flops and start pulling on a sock.

"Yeah, I think Blake's going to second and Mike's filling in at catcher. We should be good. There's Blake now." Robbie gestures with his head while he leans forward and stretches his arms behind his back.

Blake's Jeep pulls into the space next to my truck. I'm happy I'm not the only one who has missed most of practice. Blake and I have a lot in common, including our propensity for arriving fashionably late. Blake's my height, and while his hair borders on black compared to my brown, we occasionally get mistaken for brothers.

"You wanna throw?" Robbie asks, as I finish lacing up.

"Yeah." I grab my glove and the two of us toss the ball along the sideline until Blake joins us.

"Is Mallory making it out to the game tonight?" I ask Blake as he lines up next to me.

He stretches his right arm across his chest and then switches to the other one. "I doubt it. She has to watch her niece and I don't think she wants to bring her out."

We never get many fans at our games. Blake's girlfriend is the most frequent but even her appearances have gotten rare. I keep inviting people, but apparently Wednesday nights are more highly valued elsewhere. *Can't remember the last time a girlfriend of mine made it out to a game. Three seasons ago? Four? I suppose managing to keep one longer than a few months might help.*

Carson pitches us each a bucket of softballs, and I knock the majority of mine toward an increasingly dark right field. We ignore the clouds as much as possible and concentrate on practice. Once everyone has hit, we mill around the dugout, stretching, while Carson gives me his appraisal of our chances.

"These guys should be cake for us. I watched them play last week. I think we're going to crush 'em."

I consider the big athletic guys filling the opposing dugout and realize that Carson might be overly optimistic, but I don't argue. "We're definitely due for a win."

Carson starts jotting down the lineup. He's full of energy today. I admire that about him. At twenty-five, he's a little younger than me, but about a year older than Blake. He has no trouble organizing things like this. Sports are his arena. He's naturally talented at all of them. I could outrun him. Blake could out-swim us both, but Carson has everybody beat on all-around athleticism. He makes a great shortstop in any case. The other teams have learned to fear both his fielding abilities and his trash talking skills. Blake and I flank him on the field at second and third base respectively.

We walk out to our positions and are waiting for Robbie to throw the first pitch, when a thunderclap rumbles through the clouds. The umpire casts a quick glance skyward, but then yells, "Batter Up!"

I'm digging my cleats into the dirt at third when I notice my friend Francesca walking up from the parking lot. She catches my eye and sticks her tongue out at me before sitting down next to Paul, our designated hitter. I scowl at her and she laughs, and then turns to greet Paul.

What do you know? We did manage a fan tonight.

The crack of the bat jerks my attention back to the game as the ground ball takes a bad hop a few feet in front of me and impacts me in the chest. It drops to the ground and I scramble to bare hand it, making the throw to first just a step ahead of the runner. I rub my chest as I walk back to my position. *That'll be a bruise tomorrow.*

Robbie walks the next batter as I start to feel the first few drops of rain. The third batter grounds to Blake at second. He underhand tosses the ball to Carson who tags the base and hurls it to first for a double play, just as a bolt of lightning flashes beyond right field. Carson's yell of success over the play is drowned out by the boom of thunder. I head for the dugout, hoping we'll get a chance to hit, but as the outfielders come trotting in, they're followed by a dense wall of rain. I step into the dugout before the heavy drops can soak me.

"Hey Fresca, What's shakin'?" I plop down next to Francesca on the bench.

"I finally make it to one of your games and this is how you treat me?" She gestures to the sheets of rain now sweeping the field.

"I ordered you sunshine and double rainbows, but they must not have gotten the memo."

"I was worried I was going to get arrested getting here, too. Did you see all those cop cars downtown?"

I think about it for a second, then remember the newscast. "It's probably all that trial stuff going on."

"Oh, right." She turns to Blake as he sits down next to me and props his feet on the bucket of balls. "Hey, Blake."

"Hey, Francesca. Thanks for coming."

"Looks like I'll be witnessing your drinking skills instead. Are you all heading to Ferg's now?"

"I think we're going to see if this passes first." I watch the puddles building on the field.

Carson dashes back into the dugout from his conference with the umpires and drips all over the equipment as he explains the situation. "We're on delay for now. They're going to see how wet the field gets."

I play along with his optimism. Most of our team has already gone to their cars to wait, but I'm not in any hurry to leave the company of my friends. I can tell that this storm isn't likely to be over fast. Anyone with a few years of Florida weather experience gets to know the difference between a passing shower and a prolonged storm, and this one appears to be settling in for the evening. I'm bummed to not be playing for another week, but even rainout beers are better than being at work.

"I guess those guys don't think it's going to let up," Robbie says, noting the opposing dugout clearing out.

Carson picks up his clipboard. "If it stops and they don't have enough players to re-take the field, we win by forfeit."

"I came here to play. I hate winning by forfeit," Robbie grumbles.

"What's new with you, Blake?" Francesca steers the conversation away from our glum prospects.

"Did Ben not tell you the news yet?"

"No, he's obviously slacking in the gossip department. What's your news?"

Blake looks at me. "Should I show it to her?"

"You have it with you?"

"Yeah, it's in my Jeep."

"What is it?" Francesca's curiosity is piqued.

"Be right back." Blake gets up, walks past Carson, who is in deep concentration over the stats sheet, and dashes into the rain toward the parking lot.

"What's he got?" Francesca brushes a strand of dark hair out of her eyes.

"It's impressive." I grab my flip-flops out of the overhead cubbies and start changing out of my cleats.

A minute later, Blake dashes back into the dugout holding a plastic bag. He sits next to Francesca and unwraps the package, revealing a jewelry box.

"Oh for Mallory?" Francesca exclaims. Blake pries open the lid and displays the diamond ring inside. "Ooh, you did good Blake!" Francesca takes the box and looks adoringly at the ring.

"Well, it's time," he replies.

"How long have you two been dating now? Four years?" Carson's interest in the statistics sheet is waning.

"Yeah, I wanted to wait till she finished grad school, but now that she's almost done, we're taking the leap."

"That's awesome, man." Robbie pats Blake on the shoulder.

We pass the ring box around, admiring it as the rain beats down on the dugout. Under the bright lights of the baseball diamond, the ring sparkles even more than the last time I saw it. *Mallory's going to love it. I need to find a ring like that. I need to find a girl like that.*

I close the ring box and pass it on to Robbie. As I do, an exceptionally bright lightning bolt sears across the sky and hits what can only be a few blocks away. The thunderclap is deafening and immediate. The bench is a symphony of expletives and Francesca clenches my arm and pulls herself against me.

"Holy shit that was close!" Robbie says.

A high-pitched whine like a jet engine begins to emanate from the direction of the strike. It grows louder and is followed by an explosion of bright blue light that domes up through the rain and illuminates the cloudy sky.

"What the hell—" is all that escapes my mouth, before a deafening bang from a transformer blowing behind us drowns me out. I'm still too startled from the shock to move when the severed end of a power line whips into the end of the dugout and lands on the far end of our bench. The last thing I sense before blacking out is the sight of my friends glowing with a pale blue light, and the sound of Francesca screaming.

Chapter 2

"If you meet experienced time travelers, you can usually trust that they are intelligent. The nature of this business rapidly weeds out the morons."

-Excerpt from the journal of Dr. Harold Quickly, 2110.

I open my eyes to bleary but bright sunlight. I'm lying on my back staring at a clear blue sky. The bright light worsens the ache in my head, so I close my eyes again. I can feel the heat of the sun on my face and the dry itchy feeling of grass on my arms and the backs of my ears. There's definitely something crawling on my arm, but I'm too unmotivated to care. I monitor the slow progression of little insect feet, trying to gauge the threat. *Lady bug maybe? Spider?* I consider the most likely candidates. *Shit, if it's a fire ant, there's probably a zillion more around.* I open my eyes and angle my head slowly upward, trying to locate the intruder in the crook of my elbow. My eyes adjust to the light and I make out the ant. Not a fire ant. I lay my head back and stare at the midday sky. *Why is it daytime?*

Continue this story now.
https://books2read.com/in-times-like-these

ACKNOWLEDGMENTS

Tomorrow Detective was a challenging book to write and took the advice, encouragement and support of many.

My first thanks is Claire Taylor, whose Story Alignment Service gives me a sounding board for my ideas and helps shape the vision of what each book will be before I ever write the first word. It is an indispensable part of my writing process and Claire is a hero.

Alan Janney, who writes as Alan Lee, has been my guiding light in the genre of private detective fiction. Alan, I am proud to be counted among your friends. You are a daily inspiration and literate af.

I've received no end of encouragement and motivation from my fellow authors, Cecelia Mecca, Todd Hodges, Lucy Score, James Blatch, and Boo Walker. You are my ride-or-die compatriots in this writing and publishing process and your friendship makes even the tough days fun.

My team of initial readers, *The Type Pros* continues to be amazing, from spotting issues and inconsistencies to keeping me inspired. You are the names I have in mind while writing every draft. I love knowing your eyes will be the first to see the book and you will help me make it shine.

Specific thanks to: Andrew Freeman, Marilyn Bourdeau, Steve Bryant, Felicia Rodriguez, Maarja Kruusmets, Judy Eiler, Claire Manger, Mark Hale, Eric Lizotte, Alissa Nesson, Ken Robbins, Yvonne Mitchell, Bethany Cousins, Elaine Davis, and Ginelle Blanch.

Much of this novel was written at a window table at Banyan Cafe. A warm thank you to Hernan, Casey, Melissa, Jake, Kate, Carlos, Lisa, and Kayleigh, who make me feel welcome every day and do a wondrous job of keeping me motivated and caffeinated. You are my people.

And to my loving family.

You are still my favorite.

Nathan Van Coops lives in St. Petersburg, Florida on a diet comprised mainly of tacos. When not tinkering on old airplanes, he writes heroic adventure stories that explore imaginative new worlds. He is the author of the time travel adventure series *In Times Like These*, and *Paradox PI*, as well as *The Skylighter Adventures*. His recent series, *Kingdom of Engines* explores a swashbuckling alternate history where the modern and medieval collide.

Get a free book at https://BookHip.com/PMZANPS

Cover Design by Damonza

Author photo by Jennie Thunell Photography

Ebook ISBN: 978-1-950669-20-2

Paperback ISBN: 978-1-950669-19-6

Hardcover ISBN: 978-1-950669-21-9

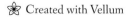 Created with Vellum

Made in the USA
Thornton, CO
02/03/23 23:07:38